Murray Gilchrist

A Peakland Faggot

Tales told of Milton Folk

Murray Gilchrist

A Peakland Faggot
Tales told of Milton Folk

ISBN/EAN: 9783744776813

Printed in Europe, USA, Canada, Australia, Japan

Cover: Foto ©Andreas Hilbeck / pixelio.de

More available books at **www.hansebooks.com**

A Peakland Faggot:

Tales told of Milton Folk

By R. MURRAY GILCHRIST

Author of "The Stone Dragon,"

etc., etc.

LONDON: GRANT RICHARDS
9 HENRIETTA STREET
COVENT GARDEN, 1897

Philemon : After I departed from you, and had taken my leave of my most sweet old mother, and of my other dear friends, I travelled into Derbyshire, and from thence into the Peak, whither I appointed my books and my clothes to be brought.

Eusebius : Into the Peak ? Lord God, what made you there? That is a marvellous and a barren country, and, as it is thought, such a country that neither hath learning, nor yet one spark of godliness.

.   .   .   .

Theophile : I think you found there very peakish people.

Philemon : Not so ; I confess that I found there very good wits, and apt unto learning.

THOMAS BECON'S *Jewel of Joy.*

TO MY FRIEND

LARNER SUGDEN

The Author thanks the Editors of *The Speaker* and *The Sunday Chronicle* for permission to republish the following sketches.

CONTENTS

A STROLLING PLAYER

A

A STROLLING PLAYER

AT the bend of the hill-road, where one loses sight of the distant village, a stream had overflowed before the last frost, and, the limestone cart-way, with its smoothly-worn cobbles and its lattice of red and yellow and black leaves, was covered for many yards with a transparent sheet of ice. In daylight it resembled a mosaic of arabesque device, but now, reflecting the last scarlet shred of the afterglow, it suggested a river of blood. All around grew dwarf sycamores and elms and silver birches; their bare timber streaked with ribbons of frozen sleet.

When the waggon reached this perilous place, Joe Ascham got down from the high shaft, and, with a few sad clucks of encouragement, strove to make the young white horse proceed. Its shoes had not been sharpened, however, and at the first attempt it slipped back with such violence that the thing inside the waggon was jolted roughly against the side. At the sound the old man winced and crept to the back and drew the burden again into the middle, covering it neatly with the strip of clean sacking.

"Theer munna be a scrat on et," he muttered,

" else Johanna 'll breek her heart altogether.   Ef et 's all reet, hoo 'll be pleased, poor soul, for et 's th' best whöak I 've ever seen !   Dane said as et cem off one o' th' big trees i' Whetstone Dale."

He caught the bridle again and pulled with all his might, and the horse felt its way very slowly, without lifting its hoofs from the ground.   The road turned abruptly again, at a corner with a steep and barren acclivity on the right hand, and on the left a dangerous ravine filled with ancient firs and rough stones.   The wind was rising, and the place seemed full of whispers.

There the horse slipped for the second time, and the sacking fell in a heap at the back.   In the waning light was visible a short and narrow coffin, with a bright metal name-plate.   Joe covered it again, and jerked the bridle almost furiously, but the horse would not move.

" O Boxer, my lad, dunna fail me at such a time," he cried, querulously.   " Johanna 's waitin' theer all alone, an' we 're late enaa already !"

Some one rose from the low wall and came towards him.   His eyes were wet, and he could only distinguish the outline of a woman's figure.

" Can I help you at all ?" she inquired, in a thin, eager voice.

" I 'ld tek et very kindly, mam, ef yo 'ld set inside an' howd et i' position.   I dunna want et spoilin'.   I could mek Boxer go, ef on'y I werena afeard o' shakin' et."

" What is inside ? " she said, lifting her bundle and preparing to climb.

" Et 's a coffin, mam . . . my poor Michal's—my dowter's."

The woman shivered, but got in without a word and knelt and clasped her arms about the thing. Joe dragged Boxer forward, and in a few minutes they had reached the level. There the woman rose to alight ; but the old man put out his hand.

" I reckon yo 're goin' my way over th' moor," he said. " Et 's five mile to my house—midway across, an' yo 're welcoom to ride ef yo' will."

She thanked him. " I want to reach Great Hucklow to-night, if I can," she said. " I 'm a strolling player, and I 'm trying to get an engagement with Bainbridge's company. I shall be very glad to ride with you, for I 've walked ever since daybreak."

Darkness fell and the air grew thick with the oncoming of snow. Ascham struck a match and lighted his lantern and walked on in front. The woman saw that they had reached the moorland : on either side was a low bank of heather-covered turf, broken here and there with frozen water holes. A few ragged sheep followed in the wake of the waggon. The road was no longer of limestone, but of brown sand and pebbles ; the shadow of the wheels stretched behind and broke amidst the moving sheep.

A few snowflakes fluttered downwards. Ascham

stopped the horse and came again to the side. The woman was still crouching with her arms about the coffin.

" I reckon et were a strange thing o' me to ask," he said, " but yo' see I were baffled. Et's getten' mortal cowd. I've got th' horse rug i' front,—yo' may 's well put it on an' sit on the shaft. Yo'll hev to step daan first."

She obeyed. He put the lantern on the ground and found the rug. He saw that she was very wan and exhausted. Her face was a wasted oval ; the skin about her eyes was blue with weeping and sleeplessness. She wore a shabby black silk cloak, trimmed with moth-eaten fur ; the hat that shaded her forehead was of dingy yellow lace. She might have been any age between thirty-five and fifty.

When Joe had pinned the rug over her breast, he helped her to the shaft and she sat there with her feet dangling. The snow was falling heavily now ; the sheep had retreated to the hollows, and even the sides of the road were invisible. Suddenly the old man lagged and fell behind to walk beside the stranger.

" I want to talk, mam," he said. " I want to forget things. Yo've seen misfortun', hevna yo'."

" Yes, I've seen misfortune," she replied. " So much misfortune that I wish the coffin had been made for me. But all of us have our share. Do you go much farther ? "

" Abaat a mile, but I 'd liefer yo' cem' up to th' haase wi' me. I dessay et 'ld do Johanna good. An' happen—ef I may tek' th' liberty o' askin' yo' —we could carry th' coffin in betwixt us."

The woman nodded.

" Ay, et 's Michal 's coffin, an' Michal 's aar on'y child. Such a rare wench too hoo were afore hoo went away. But such were her will, an' there were no howdin' her in a' whöam. Yo' should hev seen her! Hoo were just as pink an' white as th' inside o' a peony-pod. An' et were a bad year wi' th' crops, though things bettered afterwards. . . . Hoo wouldna coom whöam till a month ago, an' then hoo were heavy wi' trouble."

He was obliged to go forward again : a track, diverging to the right, crossed a frozen brook and climbed, between stunted hedges, to the farm-stead. He turned the horse safely and came back.

" I want to ask you something," the woman said, anxiously. " When she came back to you— were you kind ? "

" Kind, mam ? Ay, that we were. Et were th' happiest an' yet th' saddest day o' aar lives. Prethee wheer else should hoo hev' gone, ef none to her own fowk ? Hoo browt shame wi' her, but hoo were Johanna's dowter, an' my dowter, an' th' shame were all forgi'en."

The woman's eyes swam in scalding tears : she pressed her hands over her heart ; then she quaked, remembering a casting from a door and a shouting of curses.

A dog barked softly. The wind was whirling the snowflakes in wreathed columns that passed in front of the house like veils of smoke. From the window of an upper room a clear streak of light stretched over the croft. The dog came bounding from a shippon and jumped up to Ascham's waist.

"Hush, Gyp, we munna hev a noise," he said, stooping to stroke its head.

He "put up" the horse, leaving the stranger standing in the open air; then he unlatched a door in that side of the house that abutted on the stable-yard, and beckoning her to help, silently drew the coffin from the waggon. They carried it through the kitchen, not without difficulty, for the oak planks were thick, and into the house-place, where they laid it on the lang-settle.

Ascham went to the foot of the stairs. "Johanna," he called, gently. "I've gotten back, an' theer's a lady coom wi' me—hoo's bin helpin' me wi' et."

Mrs Ascham came down very slowly. She was a stout little woman, with clear blue eyes and brown wrinkled skin. The outline of a goitre showed through her black and white neckerchief. She held out a cold hand.

"Et were good o' yo', mam," she said. "I were afeared my lad couldna manage et by himsen."

" Th' lady's an actress," Joe explained, " on th'
way to Greet 'Ucklow. Hoo held th' coffin for
me when Boxer slipped."

Johanna tried to unbutton the ragged silk cloak,
but the stranger held it more tightly together.

" Lend me a lantern," she said, " and let me go
on. If I am not there early to-morrow, my chance
will be lost."

The old woman threw open the window. The
snowfall had thickened; it came down so quickly
that it seemed as if a white sheet hung outside.

" Yo' see et 's impossible, mam," she said. " Yo'
mun stay wi' us an' hev soom o' Joe's supper.
Th' way 's hard to find i' broad dayleet, an'
to-neet, e'en my lad, who 's lived here all his life,
wouldna dare to venture. Yo' dunna wish to
freeze to dëath ? "

The player smiled painfully. " It would not
matter much," she replied ; " but if you will have
me stay I must do something. Is there any sewing—I am good with my needle."

" No, mam, nothin'. I med shroud an' all
mysen,—i' fact they were th' very things I 'd put
by for when my own time cooms. Thank yo' very
kindly, but all 's doon."

Her husband drew her attention to the coffin.
She examined it carefully, feeling the polish of the
wood and the weight of the metal handles with
divers murmurs of pleasure.

" Et 's a beautiful thing," she remarked, at last.

"Ah, ef on'y aar Michal could see et, hoo'd be more nor satisfied!"

She took from the oven a huge bowl of hot porridge. Joe drank buttermilk with his share, but Johanna poured over the stranger's a jugful of rich cream. After supper, man and wife began to wrangle soberly concerning which should sit up in the death chamber. Johanna had done so on the preceding night, but knowing that her husband was weary with the journey, she wished to take his turn.

The actress broke in, during a pause, with—"Let me watch with your dead. I will keep awake all night."

It was only with considerable difficulty that she prevailed. Johanna told her that it had been the custom of the family for many generations.

"Michal's th' third I've watched," she said, proudly. "Theer were Joe's mother first, an' then my own lad as died thretty year ago. But Joe an' I'm growin' old an' worn aat, an' et 'll be best for us to sleep, for to-morrow 'll be a hard day. . . . What may your name be, mam?"

"Call me Violetty; that is the name my parents gave me—a foolish name, like tinsel and sawdust."

Johanna opened the staircase door. "Coom, then, Violetty," she said. "This es th' way to Michal's chamber."

She led her up the broad, worm-eaten stairs to a great room, where stood a large four-post bedstead, hung with blue and white gingham. She drew the curtains aside reverentially, and after removing a crochetted cloth, showed Violetty the face of a young girl, whose long glossy hair spread from the frilled nightcap in strands over the pillow. Johanna peered into Violetty's hollow eyes before drawing down the counterpane and showing her the baby lying in its embroidered gown, like a doll, with its head resting between the mother's left breast and arm.

Violetty's face worked ; she turned aside.

"Esna hoo a pretty yen?" Johanna said. " Twenty-one year, but et 's just as ef' hoo were ten or 'leven, an' hoo 'd gone to sleep wi' her moppet."

There was a low fire on the hearth. She put on a dried peat and turned up the lamp.

" Yo' wunna be scared, Violetty? Hoo never did ony harm to onyone. My owd man an' me 'll sleep wi' aar door ajar—et 's just across the landin'. Ef yo' want owt, yo' need but call, for I warrant yo' we shanna sleep heavy to-neet."

Violetty sat quietly in the arm-chair, with her hands folded in her lap. The old people went to bed soon : she heard them undress, and for a while caught sounds of sobbing and whispering. When they were asleep the silence of the place became too oppressive, and she walked to and fro, looking at the pictures that covered the walls. Most of these were sombre-hued chap-paintings, done on thin glass: the scene of Nelson's death hung above the funeral of Pitt, and a ruined castle surrounded by a moat beside a basket of impossible flowers. Over the mantel was a sampler, embroidered in faded silks — a prim cottage with a formal garden, on whose lawn was wrought a verse from the dialogue of *Death and the Lady*.

Soon she drew her chair to the bedside and took away Michal's face-cloth.

"If only I were dead instead of you, poor child," she said. "I have nobody and you had those who needed you."

She folded her hands again and sat gazing at the curves of the girl's body. A clock downstairs struck hour after hour; the muffled wind stroked the windows with snow. A feeling of content filled her now; it was like a dream—a dream of quietness and rest. Her life had been one long turmoil of excitement and of shame and of repentance. Michal had known only one short sorrow; hers had been many and protracted through years and years.

"There is no rest but death," she murmured.

Yet, all the time, her heart was craving for warmth and peace. She wished no longer for love: all that desire was burned out long ago: all that she wanted was a perfect calm.

The wind fell and a grey dawn broke. She heard the old couple stir in their bed, then fall asleep again. The nights of watching before and after Michal's death had taken away all their strength. She did not waken them, although she knew that unless she reached Great Hucklow before noon, all her chance of an engagement would be lost. But she felt no pang for herself, for were they not oblivious of all their trouble.

At last Johanna came, half-dressed, into the chamber. She leaned over Michal's uncovered face and kissed it twice.

"My dear deary," she whispered. "Thy nose were always cowd; et doesna seem as thou wert dëad. An' i' a little while thou 'lt be put away fro' thy owd mother."

She beckoned Violetty to follow her down to the house-place.

"I mun ask yo'r pardon," she said; "but we slept on an' on. Why didna yo' waken us? I 'm afeared yo 'll be too late. Yo 'd best stay till noon an' go wi' us to Highlow for the buryin', et 's on th' way to Greet 'Ucklow. Theer 'll be none theer —we wanted to put her away by aarsens. Besides, we hevna ony frien's."

Joe came downstairs soon and they breakfasted in silence, then Violetty, seeing that he wished to take the coffin upstairs, took hold of the end. Johanna followed, and between them they lifted Michal and the child by the towels that were spread underneath, and spread the gimped cotton-wool evenly from head to foot.

"We mun start at twelve," Joe said. Parson 'll be waitin' at two. Et 'll be a white buryin'."

He raised the lid. Violetty left them to say their last good-bye, and waited downstairs. At noon the waggon started, with the two women sitting on either side of the coffin, whilst Joe rode on the shaft. The father and mother had donned rusty black garments and big, half-mouldy gloves. Violetty still wore her silk cloak, but Johanna had lent her an uncouth scuttle bonnet that almost concealed her haggard face. The track was deep with snow, but at even distances the heads of roughly-chiselled boundary stones kept them from straying on the moor. Johanna, who held the actress's hand in hers, wept silently all the way.

When they reached the churchyard, which lies in a hollow at the end of a scattered hamlet, they found the clergyman waiting in the porch. Two gravediggers came forward to carry the coffin, but the Aschams and Violetty lifted it themselves and laid it on the trestles in front of the altar. None of the villagers were present: they knew but little of the moor-folk, and it was much too cold to venture out of doors for such a trivial sight. The clergyman's voice rang hollow amongst the stuccoed arches. Joe and Johanna trembled as if ague-struck.

The grave had been newly dug: Violetty saw on the mound, not yet covered by the falling snow, some little white bones and the shreds of a

long-decayed coffin. It was all that remained of
the boy that Johanna had lost thirty years before.
The player buried her badly-shod feet in the snow
and covered these relics hurriedly, so that they
might not hurt the mother's eyes. In a few
minutes the service was over, and ere the gravediggers began to throw back the soft clayey soil,
Violetty drew the old people away.

When Johanna had got into the waggon, Violetty
leaned over the side and kissed her.

"Good-bye," she said. "God bless you for
your comfort of me."

Johanna threw her arms around her neck.

"I wunna let yo' go, Violetty, wench," she
wailed. "Coom whöam wi' Joe an' me—coom
an' stop wi' us for good. Aar Michal 'ld hev
wished et."

Joe put his hand over his eyes. "Ay, dunna
leave us, Violetty. We 'n got nob'dy left us."

Violetty turned faint ; everything reeled before
her eyes. Then she flushed as if overcome by
some great and unexpected happiness, and clam-
bered into the waggon.

THE GAFFER'S MASTERPIECE

B

GAFFER'S MASTERPIECE

THE masterpiece was finished, and the gaffer sat in a rush-bottomed chair beside the table and gazed upon it with greater love in his eyes than had sparkled there when he had beheld his first-born. For his children had favoured their mother, who had been a managing woman—almost a shrew—and as they had grown to maturity he had become of less and less account. Long ago, even the youngest had passed into the world and all had forgotten him, save at Wakes' time and Christmas, when, out of their prosperity, they sent sparse gifts.

But the masterpiece was his own, his very own, the offspring of his body and his soul. He had stolen long hours from his rest for its creation ; all the coppers that he had saved out of his week's earnings had been spent on materials ; in fact, he had denied himself the luxury of twist so that everything might be of the best. On Saturday afternoons he had plodded to the market town to buy oddments of plain and gaily-coloured glass and bright paints and blocks of cork and dyed mosses.

19

Now that his first joy in its completion was over, he fell into a half-melancholy humour. The work was too good for him; he had owned nothing good in his life.

"I 'm jealous as someone 'll want to tek' thee away," he said, sadly, "tek' thee away an' put thee i' a peep-show. An' wheer shall I be wi'aat thee? Et 's like enaa mony 'll fancy thee; for theer 's none been such a gran' mesterpiece doan i' th' Peak i' man's mem'ry!"

He rose, and opening a door in the press, took out a red and purple table-cloth, which he spread, as carefully as his trembling fingers would permit, over the masterpiece. Before it was covered, a knock sounded on the door and the latch was lifted and an elderly matron entered. She was the hostess of the *Forester's Arms* at Milton, and, having been a schoolmate of the gaffer's eldest daughter, she considered it her duty to concern herself occasionally in his doings.

He pushed forward an arm-chair. She drew off one of her loose kid gloves, and passed her forefinger over the seat before trusting her black silk skirt to its tender mercies.

"No offence, Mester Rowarth," she said, in a thin, high-pitched voice, "but men's ways arena as women's ways, an' I 'm sore afeard o' dust wi' these ruchin's. Haasoe'er theer isna ony."

"I try to keep et as clean as I can, but et 's onpossible, wi' them purgatories on th' harstone,

to keep ashes fro' flyin'," he remarked, pointing
to the grate beneath the fire.   "Yo're lookin'
well, Ruth."

"Ay, I'm well enaa, but th' pull up th' hill's
a bit more nor I care for. . . . I've coom to
see th' mesterpiece; fowk hev bin talkin' abaat
et for God knows haa long, an' as yo've ne'er
shown et to nob'dy, I mun ask yo' for owd time's
sake."

The gaffer reddened.   "I didna want to
exhibit et afore et were finished," he said,
apologetically.   "Et's took nigh on two years
to mek, an' on'y last neet did I gie 'et th' last
touch.   Et's set naa, an' I'm willin' for everybody as cares to see.   Would yo' mind liftin'
th' cloth—very lightly—for I'm a bit uplifted,
an' my fingers arena stiddy."

She obeyed, and uncovered the masterpiece
and gave a cry of pleasure, and a low hum such
as a bee makes in a cowslip clump.

"Et's just marvellous," she said.   "All Milton
Dale an' Village true to natyure."

The gaffer stood proudly erect.   "I med et all
mysen, Ruth, wench," he said.   "When I were
a lad, I were good at workin' wi' coork, buildin'
haases an' castles an' the like, an' th' summer
afore last I were that lonesome, I tuk to et onct
more.   Every morn I went out at sunbreak an'
studied th' spot an' set et daan i' my mind, so as
at neet I could just work et aat.   Th' cottages es

med' o' coork, wi rëal rye-grass thack. I've
covered th' church top wi' lead, just as et es
covered, an' put stained glass i' th' windows.
Them beech trees wes hard to do, but I reckon
I've copied 'em well. See, theer's th' cross
again' th' big gate, an' every tomb as es o'
consequence."

He touched a corner of the churchyard where
an ancient yew thrust out uncouth boughs.
"An' theer's wheer I'm to be buried," he murmured. "Mother and feyther were laid theer,
but my wife rests wi' her own fowk at Great
'Ucklow. Esna et fine?"

Ruth Pilkington nodded. "I've just got an
idea," she said. "Et's th' rent dinner to-
morrow, why none bring et daan to th' inn an'
show et to th' party? Et'll gi'e 'em a seet o'
pleasure, an' let 'em know whatten an' owd man
like yo' es capable o' doin'. Coom early an' hev
a bit o' summat wi' me, afore th' table's set.
Milton fowk 'll be praad o' such a thing."

He laughed feebly, like an ailing boy. None
had thought him worthy of note before; he had
been simply an old stonebreaker, akin to the
beasts that had passed him on the road.

"I'll coom, Ruth, wench, an' thank yo' kindly
for askin' me."

"Yo're welcoom. Now I mun be off. Dunna
be later nor twelve. Good e'en."

He sat up all night with his masterpiece. It

is true that he undressed and moved towards the
bed, but he could not find the heart to lie down,
and he drew back immediately and went downstairs, and with a thin blanket wrapped round his
knees, sat feasting his eyes on the model. Soon
after daybreak he donned his best clothes, which
had only been used for funerals and were creased
ineradicably and moth-eaten, and went to the
overseer and begged a full day's holiday—the
first he had wanted in thirty years. Then he
returned and sat again beside the table, not
moving thence until the church clock struck
eleven.

At the appointed time he reached the *Forester's
Arms* and showed his work to a crowd of labourers
who were assembled for the mid-day drinking.
The natives of Milton have strong enthusiasms,
and their praise exhilarated the genius so much
that he could scarce touch the bountiful food
that Ruth had provided.

Soon afterwards a wild fit of terror came over
him. As he moved to the club-room, carrying
the model on a large tray, a half-drunken tramp
came from the bar-parlour. He bore a pewter
tankard, brimful of ale, which he was about to
drink on the bench outside the porch.

"Eh, mister!" he exclaimed. "What a gay
little thing—all trees an' roofs an' windows an'
chimneys. I warrant et's rain-proof."

He raised the tankard and poured some froth

on the church steeple. The gaffer cowered over his masterpiece as a hen cowers over her chicks when the harrier is near.

"I'm on'y an owd chap," he sobbed. "Eighty an' one year——"

But Ruth Pilkington caught the fellow by the shoulders and pushed him to the door, and left him cursing there, for all the ale was spilt on the sanded floor.

"Dunna fret, Mester Rowarth," she said. "Et'll wipe off—here's a bit o' soft rag. Naa set et daan on th' sideboard. Theer, et do look han'some!"

The rent agent and the farmers entered, and before they sat to the table all examined the masterpiece. Most of them were untravelled men, and the model was beyond anything they had ever seen. The height of the gaffer's triumph was when the agent shook his hand and called him "a wonderful artist," and asked leave for his wife and daughters to call at the cottage.

Whilst they dined, he leaned over the masterpiece and wondered if anything could be improved. The sundial on the chancel wall seemed slightly awry, and he determined to raise one side a hair's-breadth. The agent invited him to take wine with him, and he sipped nervously from the thick-stemmed glass.

It was evening when he left the *Forester's*

Arms. The intoxication that had followed the unaccustomed drinking had passed, but he was strangely drowsy, and when he had passed the stile that opened to the heath on whose farther side his home lay, he covered Milton Dale and Village with his neckerchief, sat down and fell asleep.

And whilst he slept the tramp, bemused and still rankling with the contumely Mrs Pilkington had thrust upon him, reeled that way. He saw the foolish genius and prepared to kick him with his iron-shod toe, but recognising the grey head and withered cheeks, he refrained.

"Why, here's th' fellow as I met at th' pub, an' here's his dommed Noah's Ark! I'll pay him aat. Et were his faut as th' —— laid her paws on me!"

He snatched off the cover, and laughed evilly as he saw the quaint workmanship of the masterpiece.

"I set two barns afire last back-end," he muttered, "an' now I'll burn a whoal village."

He struck a match and lighted the yew in the corner of the graveyard. It blazed up instantly. He whistled, for he had the soul of Nero. Then he crept behind the hedge and watched.

The gaffer woke when the church fell in ruins. He whimpered at first, but soon was silent. When the last spark had died he rose and clasped his forehead and tottered homewards.

LADY GOLIGHTLY

LADY GOLIGHTLY

ON the sideboard in the little parlour of the *Newburgh Arms* stood a tall glass case which contained a stuffed monkey. The creature wore a wreath of faded roses on her head, and on her body a tinsel bodice cut very low at the neck and a many-pleated skirt of dingy white tulle. From her waistband hung, suspended by a cord of crimson silk, a toy fan and a pasteboard puff-box, and her right hand held stiffly a funeral card, with the inscription :—

LADY GOLIGHTLY. AGED FIVE YEARS.

This lovely bud, so young and fair,
Called hence by early doom,
Just came to show how sweet a flower
In Paradise might bloom.

It was Dick Mather, the host, who told me the story. He had been fidgetting in and out of the room for some time, waiting for the inevitable inquiry. My silence brought a fretful and impatient look to his fat, rosy face, and at last he confronted me angrily.

"Why dunna yo' ask abaat her?" he said. "Theer hesna e'er bin a strange chap i' th' haase afore as didna start agate o' her th' first minute!"

I could scarce refrain from laughing. "I was only trying your patience," I replied. "It has been almost as amusing to see you as to see the monkey. What will you take?"

"Yo're a roguish un, mester, yo' are, mekin' fun o' me. Yo' see we grew that fond o' her, hevin' no childer o' aar own, an' we hed cause to be grateful to her, for et was her doin' as th' haase becem th' best payin' i' Milton. Ef fowk dunna question, et's like as ef soom sleet were meant."

"I meant none, gaffer. Come, whiskey or gin?"

"Whiskey *an*' a cigar's what I fancy most. But ef yo' treat me, I treat yo'; for et's worth money hevin' such a tale to tell."

He rang the bell and his wife, a lean, elderly dame, made her appearance.

"Whiskey an' cigars for two, loove," Dick sad.

When she had brought the tray, he lighted his cigar and set his tumbler on the mantel-shelf, and stood, splay-legged, on the fender, with his back to the fire; steadying himself ever and anon lest the weight of his protuberant chest should cause him to fall forward. He cleared his throat and prepared to begin; but suddenly his jowls shook and he quivered all over like a jelly.

"Et meks me laugh to this day," he stammered. "I'm welly scared as I'll laugh on my dëathbed, when my thowts should be set on better things!"

After a time he grew more composed, and spoke in a strained one-toned voice.

"Et were a young curate as we hed i' Milton as sow'd her to me when he were forced to gie up th' church. Poor chap, after he'd gone away, he wedded a farmer's dowter as followed him —an adder-tongued wench an' no mistake— an' 'migrated to Canady. I heerd lately as he'd gone to th' dogs!

"Yo' see, mester, he'd bin schooled i' Fraunce, at a place nigh to Paris, afore he went to college, an' he'd got into wild comp'ny theer. Drink! I 've seen him—nay, I wunna tell, for I liked him, I did, an' were main an' sorry when he cem to grief!

"He hedna bin a month i' Milton when all th' spot were gossipin' abaat him. Whey, says I, can't a fellow, though he do wear a black cöat, go innocently o' a neet fro' haase to haase for a hond at whist? Parson Firman didna approve o' et, tho', an' he grum'led till th' curate promised to mend his ways. But et on'y meant askin' fowk to his own room, 'stead o' goin' to theers! My word, he knew soom queer games! Beg-a-rat an' poker an' vantun were child's play beside soom o' em!"

"But about Lady Golightly?" I interrupted.

"I 'm comin' to et. Let me tell yo' i' my own way. Lady Golightly 's th' name for a fly-by-gy-by. We chris'ned her so when hoo cem to us. Well,

to get on, a frien' o' his sent th' monkey fro' Paris
for a Fool's Day gift, an' her tricks were that
comical as onybody 'ld gie a shillin' to see her ony-
day. Hoo could mek a cigarette, an' drink fro' a
glass like a human bein'! An' daunce—modestly
too when hoo pleased—so as ladies might hev took
lessons fro' her. A pair o' scarlet breeches an' a
coat cem wi' her, an' hoo 'd shirts an' stockin's by
th' dozen.

"Clean? Hoo were that—dainty I call her.
Everyone took to her. Ef I were to tell yo' all
her ways et would tek me till this time next
week."

Mrs Mather put her head into the parlour.

"Dick, yo 've to start for Gressbrook i' five
minutes," she said.

"All reet, loove. I see I mun cut th' story
short, mester. Hoo were th' pride o' th' better
end o' fowk, hoo were. An' naa I 'll tell yo' what
happed as caused th' curate to be turned aat.

"Parson Firman's wife were gettin' up a fancy-
fair for a new wing for th' rectory, an' knowin'
what an attraction th' poor thing 'ld be, hoo bor-
rowed her fro' the curate. An' th' young ladies
med her th' petticoat as hoo's got on naa, an' gev'
her th' fan an' th' paader box. Th' curate towt
her a new waulse, wi' her little arms put aat
loovely, an' keepin' to time quite nat'ral. I used
for to go an' watch her. Her face were that prim
as yo' wouldna hev b'lieved hoo 'd a cunnin' thowt

i' her yëad. When hoo were tired, hoo 'ld set her
daan on her stool an' fan hersen so genteel as yo 'ld
hev thowt hoo 'd a rëal soul i' her body. Such as
hoo took to, hoo 'ld coom an' set on theer knees,
an' cuddle theer neck just like a lass cuddles her
young man. . . . Yo' mun excuse me, mester,
this part o' th' tale always affects me."

He drew out a yellow silk handkerchief and
wiped his eyes and blew his nose strenuously.

"Yo' munna think I 'm 'shamed o' showin' et,"
he said, defiantly; "for I amna. Hoo were that
loovin'——"

His wife came again to the door.

"Coom, lad, th' cart's rëady. Yo'll miss meetin'
wi' th' carrier ef yo' dunna start soon."

"Ay, I 'll be off presently. Tell Jem to howd
th' tit. There 's plenty o' time."

"When he 's tellin' abaat Lady Golightly," she
remarked, in a pathetic voice, as she turned away,
"he ne'er knows when to stop. Hoo were a
greet favourite wi' us."

"Parson's dowters hed a lot o' fun wi' her, too,"
Dick continued. "More nor onct they fetched
her up to th' rectory to show to visitors, an' by
all accaants hoo were as polite as onybody theer.
Well, th' time cem for the fancy-fair, an' th'
schoolroom were decorate gran'ly wi' things hired
fro' London—owd shop-fronts an' haases wi' bal-
conies, to represent a city i' past days. Missus
an' me went in th' evenin' just afore th' enter-

c

tainment, an' I bowt her them wool-mats i' th' window bottom, an' a basket med o' alum that parson hed wrowt. Et werena worth much— when et were weshed, et melted away like snow!

"They hed a stage at th' far end, just as good as i' ony theatre, wi' scenes an' a curtain, an' footleets, an' th' pyano were lent fro' th' rectory, wi' th' eldest dowter to play.

"Th' first as performed were th' curate, who'd blecked his face an' donned a big collar like a nigger minstrel. He'd a banjo, an' he sang 'O Susanny' an' 'Th' owd fowk a' whöam' i' splendid style. After him cem Missus Firman, warblin' 'We hev lived and looved together,' but th' poor parson groaned an' glared as ef he were sayin' 'domn' to himsen. Then th' pyanist played a waulse tune, an' Lady Golightly tripped on fro' th' back, an' stood near th' leets, curtseyin' an' blowin' kisses to everybody.

"By jowks, but hoo took on! They clapped an' clapped till et seemed as ef th' ramshackle pasteboard haases 'ld all tum'le daan. When et were a bit quieter, hoo lifted her paader-box an' did her face over, an' fanned hersen, an' stood a-caantin' th' music notes, so as to know when to step in.

"Then et looked as ef hoo'd forgot th' daunce, for hoo scratted her yëad an' pondered. An' i' another moment hoo ups wi' her petticoat an' began a jig the like o' which had ne'er been seen i' th' Peak afore. I wunna tell yo' haa hoo carried on, but I heerd after as et were a *can-can,* such as they perform i' Fraunce!

"Parson's wife hoo screeted an' went off i' a sway, an' all th' gentry i' front got up an' went aat, but th' common sort i' th' sixpenny seats fairly bent double wi' laughin'. Th' best o' et were as th' curate 'peared so put aat as he hedna nerve to stop her.

"I've my daats as to who towt her. Th' curate said afterwards as he were innocent, an' as hoo mun hev hed experience on a stage afore that nect. Onyhow, he were forced to resign, an' he left Milton, an' Gill's eldest wench said he'd promised to wed her, an' hoo followed him. As I towd yo' afore, he went to th' dogs.

"I bowt Lady Golightly of him for two pun', as I were goin' to tek this public, an' hoo drew everybody here wi' her dauncin'. Hoo ne'er wanted to waulse again—like as not hoo wished to gie fowk all th' pleasure hoo could—an' et were always th' *can-can.* Hoo browt us a fine seet o' money, an' theer's a lot as cooms yet just to look at her i' her glass coffin.

"Hoo died last Kirsmas. We felt et, we did; for hoo were like a dowter to missus an' me. An' now, mester, I mun leave yo'."

A FAMILY SUPPER

A FAMILY SUPPER

MRS FIRMAN stood in the open doorway strenuously urging Emma Palfrey to be more regular in her attendance at church. The surplices were all neatly ironed and packed in the basket, ready to be carried up to the rectory. It was only from pure kindness that the parson's wife sent the linen there to be washed, for despite the fact that Emma's charges were at least as much as those of the other women, she was excessively plain of speech, and devoid of the wit to flatter.

" I 'm mostly too tired, mam," she said. " All week et 's toilin' to keep goin', an' on Sundays I 'm fit for nowt but to set i' th' easy-chair an' nod. Et 's on'y when I 'm feelin' wakeful as I dare go to hear Mester Firman."

The lady passed on to the next cottage, and Emma opened the back-door and called her brother in from the shed, in which he had hid himself at the sound of the visitor's footstep.

" Coom, Tommy, lad. I want yo' to help carry th' basket. Wesh yo'r face an' don yo'r cap."

Her voice was soft, and tender, and protecting now, just as if she spoke to an ailing child. Tommy shambled forward and stood before her

with his arms hanging limply. He was a tall,
pale man of thirty, with thin black beard and
shifty, protuberant eyes. His clothes were old,
faded with many scourings and patched with
pieces of divers colours.

" Hes hoo gone ? " he asked, timidly. " I 'm
scared when hoo looks at me ! "

" Ay, dear, hoo 's gone. Naa get rëady, an'
we 'll start."

Just then the front door opened again, and
Cousin Richard Palfrey of Watery Flat thrust
his close-cropped, bullet - shaped head into the
room. Tommy disappeared at once. Emma
clasped her thin hands fearfully. Perhaps he
had come once more to bid her send Tommy
to the Bastille. She would be firm as ever, but
the struggle would shake her, and she was no
longer strong.

An uncommon pleasantness, however, shone in
his bead-like eyes, and his nose and jowls glis-
tened unctuously.

" Haa yo' do go on, Emma," he said, jocosely.
" Yo' cast yo'rsen abaat like a rag-an'-stick play-
actress. I 'm sure yo 've no call to be nervous
wi' me."

" Yo 've always bin kind wi' yo'r advice,
Richard," she stammered. " Very kind, an'
tho' I couldna tek et, I 'm none th' less thankful."

" That 's a reet frame o' mind, owd virgin,

hee, hee! I amna coom abaat Tommy to-day—
that 'll wait a bit. Theer's more important
things to worry wi'."

" Nob'dy badly, I do trust, Richard?"

" No. Whey, yo're no hand at guessin', so I
may's well tell yo' straight aat. Uncle Silas
Pawfrey's coom ower fro' Manytoby—got to
Watery Flat last neet, an' he's med up his
mind as he mun see all his kin. I wouldna
hev bothered wi' yo', but he minds as yo'r feyther left children. We're goin' to hev' a
supper to-neet; cowd roast duck wi' trimmin's,
an' hot vëal an' pork an' black puddin's, an' God
knows what! He's a warm man, an' wi'aat
chick or child to leave et to, an' as I've always
writ to him, et's my duty to mek him welcoom.
There'll be fifteen o' us to set daan to th'
table."

The prospect made the spinster's warped
cheeks grow warm.

" Es Tommy to coom, too?"

" Ay, I towd Uncle as he were a nat'ral an'
twenty-five year younger nor yo', an' as haa
et'ld be best for him to stop a' whöam, but
Uncle's a queer chap as will hev his way. 'All
or none,' says he; so Tommy may coom, an' eat
i' th' kitchen after we've all doon. Yo' mun
get on yo'r best things an' coom up by six
o'clock, for like as not yo' can help my missus
wi' th' cookin'. Naa I mun be off."

Emma called Tommy again, and they hurried up the street with the rectory linen. When they returned she took from a chest her father's old Sunday suit of shiny grey cloth and his darned gloves and black satin stock.

" Yo' mun don quickly, Tommy lad," she said. "We 're goin' to a fam'ly supper at Cousin Richard's—th' first I 've bin to sin yo' were born. An' yo' mun be very quiet an' well behaved."

Tommy was capering about like an excited goat.

" Will theer be mëat?" he inquired.

" Ay, dear, cowd roast duck wi' trimmin's, an hot roast vëal an' pork—such things as we 've forgotten th' taste o'. Naa go to y'or chamber an' get rëady. I 'll fas'n on yo'r collar an' tie."

She unwrapped from the newspaper coverings a puce stuff gown, which she spread out on the bed, with a pair of cuffs and a chemisette of tatting that she had worn in her girlhood. Then she took off her working clothes and let down her thin grey hair, and after plaiting it in a great number of rats'-tails, she arranged it in what she called the " basket style." There was a little lavender water in the cracked smelling bottle on the mantelpiece; she pulled out the stopper and sprinkled a few drops over her cotton handkerchief.

In the mildewed glass she saw herself yellow

and wrinkled, but her heart was brave. Her comeliness had all been sacrificed for her brother's sake, and she knew no pangs of regret.

"I were none fow once," she remarked, grimly, "but et were a long while back. I reckon, though, I'll be as genteel as on'y o' my cousins' wives. Well, et'll be a trëat to see feyther's on'y brother as is left." She raised her voice, "I'm rëady, Tommy, lad. We munna be late."

He shuffled into her chamber and she buttoned his collar and fastened his stock and smoothed the ruffled beaver of the ancestral chimney-pot. Then she dismissed him and put on her Paisley shawl and her best bonnet, with the wreath of dingy apple-blossom.

They walked quickly through the village, followed by the ironical comments of the spectators. After they had left the Nether End, and climbed over the stile that led to the Watery Flat fields, Tommy's spirits became almost painfully high.

"We hevna hed ony mëat but scraps for longer nor I can rec'lect," he said, "but I'll put summat away!"

"Yo' mun be well-mannered, dear. I dunna think as Cousin Richard'll be again yo' hevin' a good bellyful on a 'casion like this, but I want yo' to do th' fam'ly credit afore Uncle Silas. He munna go away thinkin' as his brother's lad werena bred politely."

Tommy chuckled and rubbed his hands. "Ay,

I'll be good, Emma," he said. " Yo'll hev nowt
to be 'shamed o' i' me."

They reached the farmhouse and entered, as
poor relations must do, by the back door. Mrs
Richard was standing afront the fire, vigorously
basting a leg of pork. She paused at the sound
of their salutation, and turned her long red face
towards them, wiping the sweat from her brow
with her sleeve.

" Well, of all th' guys, Emma, yo' an' Tommy's
the chiefest!" she exclaimed. " Tek off yo'r
bonnet, wench, an' look to this roast. Theer's
no need for yo' to wear ony apron ower that
gown o' yo'rs."

Emma obeyed meekly. Tommy sat on a bench
by the door and poised his hat on his knee.

" I'm goin' to lay th' table i' th' haase-place,
naa," the mistress explained ; " so I'll trust yo'
to see as nowt brens. Th' comp'ny's i' th'
best parlour, and theer's as much as I can do.
Yo'll none be able to see Uncle till supper
time."

She flounced away and Emma basted until her
eyes watered. The heat and the smell of the
viands was apparently too much for Tommy, who
stole silently from the kitchen and sought a
cooler spot.

Mrs Palfrey returned after a half-hour's careful
arranging and re-arranging of pottery and glass.
She went to the pantry, and after a loud gasp,

began to scream violently. Tommy sneaked into
the kitchen again, flushed and greasy-lipped.

"I couldna help et, Emma," he whispered.
"I've het 'em."

The basting ladle fell to the hearth. Emma's
legs trembled; she nearly swooned. The best-
parlour door opened and heavily-shod feet clattered along the passage.

In another minute Richard Palfrey entered
with a horsewhip and lashed Tommy across the
face again and again.

The old maid's blood boiled suddenly. She
picked up the poker and struck her cousin with
all her might on the shoulder.

"I'll murder yo' ef yo' touch him again!" she
cried. "Try et on ef yo' dare!"

By this time the guests had entered. Richard
turned, blind with rage; but his wife had caught
Emma by the waist and was shaking her as a
terrier shakes a rat.

"Th' gawby's gone an' guttled up th' ducks!"
she hissed. "Theer's nowt but böans left, an'
Emma's welly killed Richard wi' th' potter!"

Emma's bewildered gaze fell on Uncle Silas, a
lean old man, with a big nose and a prominent
upper tooth, who bore a strong resemblance to
her father. She tore herself away and fell on
her knees and twined her fingers together.

"He couldna help et," she whimpered. "Et
were th' smell o' mëat. O Uncle, speak for us!"

But Uncle Silas, disappointed of his favourite dish, pushed her rudely aside. "Ye wicked judy," he snarled.

A few moments later brother and sister were stumbling homewards through the dusky fields. Emma had broken down for the first time in her life. She grasped Tommy's elbow with both hands, and leaned against him, sobbing bitterly.

THE PANICLE

THE PANICLE

THE farmhouse parlour faced the north, and the cold light, made dimmer by the bubbles of green glass in the heavy lattice, gave the place a grotto-like aspect. The floor, raddled round the sides, and covered in the middle with a knitted carpet of yellow and black cloth, was made of uneven flags ; as much of the walls as was visible between the rows of memorial cards and samplers, and the engraved portraits of eminent divines, from John Wesley to James Caughey, nauseated the unaccustomed beholder with a monstrous design of livid roses, festooned with ribands of pea-green.

At the door Mrs Ollerenshaw paused and gazed inward with the devotion of one who prepares to enter a temple. She stooped and held her head sideways to discover if any dust had settled on the highly-polished, gate-legged table. Its cleanliness proving satisfactory, she folded her checked duster into the smallest compass and replaced it in the beaded bag that hung at her side, and went to the harmonium that stood between the two windows.

She was a fine, middled-aged woman, with prominent teeth, a hooked nose, and a pallid complexion. This evening she wore her most imposing gown of steel-grey poplin. As she sat on the high music stool, her back view was like that of a well-developed girl, and her dull, crimped hair seemed as luxurious as in the days when, as the Methodist local preacher's young daughter, she had caught the fancy of the wealthiest farmer of the country-side.

She played the tune of *Miles Lane*, and began to sing in a voice which, despite its Peakland accent and great unpliability, was sweet and clear and strong, a doggerel hymn written by her father in denunciation of all creeds save his own.

A maid clattered along the passage and stood waiting until Mrs Ollerenshaw had finished the second verse, which condemned superstitious fools and Unitarian and Roman Catholic fiends with equal bitterness.

"Theer's Mester Bateman Middleton coom, mam."

Her mistress rose and closed the lid of the harmonium.

"Yo' can bring him here, Libby," she said. "Be sure an' see as he wipes his feet well."

Then she sat composedly in the leather-covered arm-chair with the big legs, in which her husband had slept away his last days. She had just straightened her skirt when Bateman appeared. He was a tall, well-proportioned lad, with a broad, tanned face. He had donned for the

occasion his fawn-coloured holiday suit and his
brightest necktie. Mrs Ollerenshaw shook his
hand and made him take the chair at the other
end of the hearthrug. After they had discussed
the weather and the seed-crops, she came suddenly to the point.

"Emma towd me as yo' were coomin' up to ask
leave to coort," she said, "an' so I thowt et 'ld be
best for her to be aat o' the road. Hoo's ridden
ower to her uncle Pursglove's, and hoo's none
comin' beck till morn."

The young man's face saddened ; he had hoped
for a pleasant family scene, of the kind he had
read about in the novels of Mrs Sherwood's day,
which are still in vogue in the Peak country.
He was not uncertain of the mother's favour. There
was no complaint to be urged against his position ;
the farm of The Hallowes was his own property,
and his brood mares had won three consecutive
year's prizes at the Noe Valley Show. Emma was
his first love, and he foresaw no disappointment.

"Et's a faith-trial as I'm goin' to test yo' by,"
Mrs Ollerenshaw explained. " My feyther tried et
on my husband, an' his answer were satisfyin', an'
ef yo'rs es—then yo've my consent off-hand."

"I'm willin'," the lover replied, feebly. " Em
said et 'ld be no use aar walkin' together onless
yo' gev leave." His tone became more concilia-
tory. "Hoo's a good dowter, an' hoo'll be guided
by yo'r will."

"Well, then, et's this," said the widow. "Theer were a farmer as used to coom to aar haase when I were a wench, an' he said as it happed to his wife ere they wedded. I wunna gie my opinion o' et: soom b'lieves et an' soom doesna. . . .

"Et fell abaat this way. Th' young woman were goin' to Tidsa Market wi' butter, an' her röad lay 'cross Middleton Moor. Et were a hot forenoon i' hay-time, an' hoo were dry as a cricket, an' theer werena ony quick wayter to slake wi'. Well, hoo went on an' on, till at last hoo couldna beer et ony longer, an' hoo set daan her basket an' looked abaat. Th' Deep Rake's up theer, wheer fowk used to dig for lead i' ancient times, an' all th' pit-whöals are full o' green wayter covered wi' scum. Et were filthy, but hoo couldna forebeer, an' hoo just stooped her daan an' supped an' supped like a cawf till hoo were full. Then hoo got up, tuk her basket an' started on again, but afore hoo'd walked ten steps summat stirred abaat i' her stomach. . . . Th' owd man said as et twisted inside like a live horsehair! Th' long an' th' short o' et were as hoo didna go to Tidsa Market that day, nay, nor for long enaa afterwards. Hoo grew white an' flabby, an' i' less nor a month were that bad as hoo couldna leave whöam!"

Bateman's mouth opened. "Eh dear!" he exclaimed. Mrs Ollerenshaw sighed when she saw his consternation.

"Doctors could do nowt for her," she continued;

"an' her fowk 'gan to think hoo were deein'. At last someone suggested as th' wise man as lived Whetstone-way might be o' soom service. So they sent for him, an' he cem, an' said et were a panicle hoo 'd swallowed. A *panicle*, but yo 'll find et i' no book! An' next day at th' edge o' dark he med 'em build up th' brewhaase fire wi' fir baughs, an' then he tuk th' lass an' fas'ned her i' a chair wi' ropes, an' tied her hair to th' back-bars an' turned all aat, an' locked th' door. He kep' her afront th' fire till hoo were well-nigh roasted. Th' owd man reckoned he were lis'ning aatside an' her möans were summat fearful!

"All o' a sudden th' panicle popped ets yëad aat o' her maath an' looked raand. Then et drew back 'gain, but th' wise man hed sin et, an' he picked up th' potter as lay gain, an' shoved et into th' heart o' th' fire. But th' brute wouldna coom aat again, so he moved th' young woman till her knees welly touched th' grate. . . . Hoo were all covered wi' blisters afterwards, th' owd chap said, an' hoo hed a bad baat o' 'rysiplus. At last th' wise man saw th' panicle's yëad coom aat again, so he popped behind th' chair an' hid. An' et crawled aat, bit by bit—a bëast th' picture o' a fat effet, wi' six claws like honds, an' a swelled body abaat an arm's-length long, an' een bloodred. Et let etsel' daan to her bresses, an' afore ets tail were aat o' her maath, ets fow yëad were lyin' i' her lap. After a while et drew ets tail daan an' coiled up i' a knot. An' then, wi' one hond, th' wise man nipped up th' potter an' clapped t' other hond to th' wench's lips, an' 'gan to bren th' panicle to dëath!''

The lover's legs were trembling; his arms slipped from the sides of the chair and hung nerveless.

"O Lord! O Lord!" he ejaculated.

Mrs Ollerenshaw shook her head resignedly. She had heartily wished him to pass unscathed through the faith-trial; but she was not a woman to be soured by disappointment.

"When he touched it wi' th' potter, et writhed abaat like a bit o' crozzlin' worsted, then et stood up on ets hindmost claws an' tried to get beck, but his hond—which it bit, cowsin' him to use costick—were i' th' way, so et tumbled daan an' lay on th' harstone. . . . He set th' potter 'cross et lengthwise. . . . Et 'gan screetin' like a child. . . . But et soon were a lump o' cinder.''

A long silence followed. Bateman broke it with a tremulous inquiry.

"Did th' young woman get better, mam?"

"Th' man as towd us married her, onyhaa, Bateman.''

"I never heerd o' such a awesoom thing! I'd liefer hev died!''

Mrs Ollerenshaw rose. "So yo' b'lieve et, Bateman?"

"That I do, mam! Et's as ef I could see et naa."

"Well, I'll say good-neet to yo'. Onyone as b'lieves such a thing esna fit to wed wi' Emma."

He crept, dumfounded, from the room. She watched him pass through the garden, then, moved by some careful impulse, she followed to the door.

"Bateman," she called, "coom beck a moment!"

He returned hastily, with a glad flush driving away his wanness.

"Ay, mam?"

"On'y this, Bateman; yo' munna coom coortin' Emma ony moor."

THE GAP IN THE WALL

THE GAP IN THE WALL

IT was a hot May forenoon and the sloping
meadows were pied with anemones. Four
cuckoos were crying against each other at the
end of the hazy valley; a building magpie
castanetted incessantly from the elm planting.

Keziah Unwin was going down to Hatherton
Flat with a present of Rouen ducks' eggs for old
Mrs Pursglove. The produce of the poultry on
her father's farm was Keziah's perquisite, and she
was so accomplished in the art of rearing that her
advice was sought by all the country side. There
was no need for her to save the money she earned,
for she was the only child of a well-to-do man;
so she spent it in the purchase of good and pretty
clothes, such as raised the standard of the village
taste.

She had donned a dainty gown of pale blue linen
that clung without wrinkles to her slender figure.
A little tippet of white lace covered her shoulders.
Cousin Sarah, who had opened a milliner's shop
in the country town, had sent her that Parisian
hat which seemed like nothing but a tangle of
apple-blossom that had broken off the parent tree
and fallen prone on a cushion of emerald moss.

It was only natural that such a beautiful girl

59

should be troubled with many suitors. Swain after swain strolled into the house-place at night, ostensibly for the sake of listening to her father's old tales, but really to give themselves the wild delight of making sheep's eyes at the young mistress. She had listened to numerous offers of marriage and had declined all, and now experience had taught her how to slay a would-be lover's courage with well-planted barbs of good-natured ridicule. Local history enshrines the story of young John Hancock's proposal. Keziah revealed it to none, but the discouraged youth wailed it out at the *Bold Rodney* whilst in his cups. By unlucky stratagem having been left alone with her for a while, he began to stammer his feeble declaration. She affected great terror, but still retained enough presence of mind to enable her to pour a bucket of cold water over his head. When he became normal again she prevented a repetition of his misdemeanour with the cruel words. "Eh dear, I am glad! I thowt yo' were i' a fit!"

Once only had her heart been touched, and that was when Rafe Paramour of Rocky Edge had put the question. They had been school-mates together, and in later years had romped like hoyden and hobble-de-hoy seeking birds' nests in Milton Dale. She had begun to care for him without knowing it, but when he spoke she flouted him so mercilessly that he had withdrawn

at once. The lad had attributed her refusal to
the narrowness of his circumstances, and although
since then his love had increased, he had never
noticed her save in the coldest fashion.

At the curve of the highway where the haw-
thorns grow thickest, she paused to reflect.   If
she continued walking along the white, dusty road
she would have two miles farther to go; but if
she took a short cut, which necessitated slipping
through hedgerows and climbing rough, loosely-
built limestone walls, she could reach Hatherton
Flat in less than a quarter of an hour.

" I 'll risk et," she said.   " They 're Rafe Paramour's fields, but he wunna be abaat to-day.   I 'm
welly sweltered wi' th' heat."

So she laid the basket on the bank, and crept
between the gnarled trunks.   In another minute
she was walking leisurely on the bank of a brook,
where May-blobs and ladies'-smocks luxuriated.
At the well-head, where the water leaped from
under a block of sandstone, she turned and made
for a gateway that opened to a field of green
wheat, and skirting this she reached the first high
wall.

It was a difficult place to climb, for the ground
on the farther side was on a higher level and the
loose coping overtopped the tallest flower in her
hat.   But she was young and agile, and she did
not flinch.   She placed the egg-basket on a safe
stone and began to ascend.   It was more danger-

ous than she imagined, and the scaly limestone crumbled beneath her feet.

She had almost reached the top when her heart gave a great leap, for the wall had begun to rock with her weight. She had only just time to fling herself on the soft turf of the higher field when more than three yards of masonry fell down into the green wheat.

She rose leisurely. Despite her alarm, her flushed face bore a pleasant look of malice.

" Et 'll be a nice job for Rafe to build et up again," she said. " Ef et 'd bin onybody else's I 'ld hev towd as I 'd done et, an' paid for et too, but sin et 's his, et 'll part work out my spite."

Suddenly she gave a little scream of fear, for almost within touching distance was Rafe Paramour himself, seated beneath a full-bloomed crab and busily whittling thatch pegs. He was smiling wryly; there was something ogre-like in his aspect.

She caught up the basket, which had escaped any harm, and ran, but he sprang to his feet and followed with great strides.

" I heerd what yo' said, Keziah," he remarked, firmly, " an' I dunna think et were i' a kindly spirit. Haasoever, et 's th' custom here for him as pulls daan a wall to build et up again. An' yo 've got to do et."

She turned and faced him defiantly.

" I wunna ! "

" But yo' will, for I 'll mek yo'."

Her colour deepened. " Yo 'll be th' first man
as hes e'er med me do owt I hedna a mind to,"
she said. " Stan' aside an' let me go."

" That I shanna. Yo 're trespassin' ; dunna yo'
see yon board wi' ' Trespassers will be prosecuted '
on ? Well, I 'll prosecute yo' by mekin yo' build
the wall up."

" I 'll call aat, an' someone 'll come," she said,
half tearfully.

" Call till yo 're tired, nob'dy 'll hear. Yo' mun
just buckle to ! "

" Yo 're a brute, Rafe Paramour, to tek advantage o' me i' this way ! I werena browt up to
build walls."

He gazed at her with whimsical tenderness.
" Et 'll be a lesson for yo', Keziah : yo' humbled
my pride, and I 'll humble yo'rn. Them big
stones go first ; set to as quick as yo' like."

For the first time since her refusal of his suit
she looked full into his face. He instantly
assumed an air of great firmness. It had never
struck her before that he was very handsome,
but as he stood there without jacket or waistcoat,
and with snowy shirt all damp with perspiration,
she became convinced that there was none in
the neighbourhood half so worthy of the name of
man.

She drew off her yellow cotton gloves. There
was a suspicious quivering about her lips ; she did

not know which was nearer—laughing or crying—
and her eyes were sparkling brightly.

"I hate yo'," she murmured. "Ef I mun do
et, I mun. I doubt et 'll murder me!"

He laughed outright. "I dunna want that sin
on my conscience," he said. "I reckon I 'll hev
to let yo' off th' hardest part o' th' job. Yo' may
pick up th' least stones, an' I 'll pick up th'
biggest."

So they began to work in silence. He noticed,
with delight, that the stones she brought were
no larger than apples, and that it took her five
minutes to bring each. Neither spoke until the
first two rows were laid.

"Et 'll tek us a day at this rate," Rafe said at
last, "an' et 's dinner time now. I 've gotten
bread an' cheese an' beer under th' trees. We 'll
share et."

"What 'ld fowk say ef they knew?" she
whispered. "I wouldna do et for th' world."

"Yo' will do et," he replied, resuming his
sternness. "None 'll know fro' me."

So she was forced to obey. The bread and
cheese stuck in her throat, and she scarcely drank
from the horn. She was soon ready to return to
her work, but he made her remain at his side.

"I always hev a pipe o' bacca after meals," he
said. "Let 's chat abaat owd times. D' yo'
rec'lect me killin' a hern to get his beard for
yo'? I climbed up th' biggest tree i' Hassop

Park to pick him off th' branch wheer he'd dropped."

Keziah sullenly refused to notice his ingratiations. Soon she rose perforce, and began to collect the stones again ; this time working more diligently than before. But, somehow, the more she hurried, the more he lagged, and it was four o'clock before the gap was half-filled.

She fell a-weeping in earnest. He heard the sound, and his breath came quickly.

" Keziah, wench," he said, in a soft voice. " I think I've tried yo' enow. Yo' can go, an' I'll finish et mysen."

She took no heed ; but, hastily drying her tears, brought the stones faster than ever. Seeing that she was in such deadly earnest, he put on a spurt, and in two more hours the wall was finished.

Then Keziah took up the basket and began to walk in the direction of home. She was quite speechless, and her head hung forward almost limply. He felt afraid that he had been too hard, and overwhelming pity swayed into his heart.

He hurried after her, reaching her side before she passed through the gateway.

" Keziah," he cried. " I ask your pardon."

She set down the basket and showed him her hands. The skin was roughened, the finger-tips were bleeding. The sight made his eyes swim.

" My poor Keziah, wunna yo' forgie me ? "

E

All the shadow left her face.

" Yo 've been a wretch, but I will," she faltered. " I wunna pull yo'r walls daan again."

He came nearer, and caught her in his arms.

" I wouldna hev done et ef I hedna looved yo'."

" Et 's all reet, Rafe.   Yo 'll be master, I reckon."

And she kissed him, and he led her to the road.

BEN BAGSHAWE'S WIDOW

BEN BAGSHAWE'S WIDOW

A FEW old cronies sat in the tap-room of the *Black Bull* at Milton, sipping ale from Jubilee mugs and discussing the arrangements for Ben Bagshawe's funeral. After the ceremony the mourners were to feast in the club parlour, and Mrs Fearnehough, the landlady, was busily kneading spice-bread, which was to be baked in the wall-oven that was heated by the fire in an adjacent kitchen. Above the smell of shag and twist floated the delectable fragrance of the ducks that roasted slowly in revolving cradle-spits.

"I'll always howd et queer as a chap like Ben 'ld hang hissen," remarked a rosy old gaffer. "I mind when he were as breet an' cheerful as ony lad on the country-side. Him 'n me, though he were a cut above me, so to speak, gallassed more nor a bit together."

"Happen theer's bin a bit o' naggin' goin' on a' whōam," his neighbour hinted, darkly. "Fowk do say as th' missus——"

Mrs Fearnehough heard, and paused on her way to the oven, holding two flat cakes at arms'-length.

"Yo' munna talk i' that gait here," she said,

69

with much sternness. "I wunna hev' a word said again Mrs Bagshawe. Hoo's bin as kind a wife as could be fun'. An' surely crowner owt to know best when he says as th' poor fellow were insane."

A tall, thin man, dressed in smooth broadcloth and black gloves and hat, entered from the forecourt. He was sallow and smock-faced; and although his expression was mild to the extent of weakness, his bearing was stately and his manner commanding. He had the dignity of a good-natured Alnaschar.

"A pot o' yo'r whöam-brewed, Martha, afore I go up th' hill, if yo' please," he said. "I 'm all i' a sweat out'ardly an' dry as touchwood in'ardly wi' hurryin'. I were at brother John's i' Scarsdale, an' the letter were misdirected. I on'y heerd o' poor Ben's dëath late last neet, when theer werena a train to coom by."

"Ay, Mester Offerton, et 'ld be a sad blow to yo', bein' as yo' were th' departed's best friend."

"Et were, indeed, Martha. I s'pose yo 're goin' to hev th' buryin' tea here? Hev yo' heerd how th' widow es?"

"Keepin' up bravely. Hoo were down this morn wi' two couple o' ducks—weighin' six pun' apiece—for me to cook. I hedna ony, mysen. Et 's a wonder how hoo beers et, but hoo 'd always a fine pluck. I do b'lieve ef I 'd fun' my man a-danglin' in a barn, I'ld hev screeted mysen to dëath."

"Well, Martha, I mun be off; I'll see yo' again later. We're all to be up at Silver Cliff by two o'clock. Good day, lads."

When he was gone, Mrs Fearnehough retired to the kitchen and the idlers continued their gossip.

"Happen they'll get wed now," said the red-faced man. "Et were well known as he coorted her afore hoo took Ben. They're cousins, but hoo's six year owder nor him. A bit o' branglin' cem betwixt 'em : I dunna know what et were abaat. I've oft thowt Ben'ld hev bin welly pleasèd ef he'd hed her."

Meanwhile Francis Offerton climbed the stony lane that led to the edge-top. At the garden gate a stout, hard-featured matron welcomed him with excessive solemnity. She was a poor neighbour's wife, and her position as mistress of the ceremonies had filled her with a great sense of importance.

"Yo're late, Mester Offerton. We've been waitin' for yo' afore puttin' th' lid on. Yo' might like to look at him."

She preceded him along the hollowed path to the damp, stuccoed house, where every window was hung with white. In the hall she showed him the tray of gloves and scarves, then she led him to the parlour, where the dead man's friends stood in groups. The shining oak coffin was laid on a sheet-covered table. She removed the face-cloth.

"Th' owd gentleman's med a beautiful corpse," she said, in a hushed voice. "He were a bit purple at first—quite a nat'ral colour: et were due to suffocatin', but he's white as a lily now. An' limber" (she twitched the sharp, high-bridged nose)—"I never did see onybody so limber! They say et's a sign o' another death i' th' fam'ly. . . . Now, what 'll yo' tek,—port or sherry wine? Here's th' biscuits: yo've done reet i' choosin' port."

Barton, the Milton undertaker, and his men entered, and after them came the widow, a comely woman of fifty, attired in rich crape, and holding a deep-bordered handkerchief to her eyes. The lid was fastened down in silence, then the pall of black woollen, with its thick white fringe, was unfolded and spread over all. The gloves and scarves were distributed amongst the bearers.

"Are yo' all ready?" Barton inquired. "Reet. Two o' yo' tek th' yead, two th' middle, an' two th' foot. Carry et low down to th' gate an' rest et on th' stools as es set ready. Mrs Bagshawe, mam, yo' tek Mester Offerton's arm, him bein' th' nearest akin to yo'. Mester Andrews, tek Miss Wilkins; I 'll arrange th' rest aat o' doors."

At the gate the coffin was lifted shoulder-high—
the heavy pall and the crooked legs of the bearers
suggesting some monstrous insect—and the pro-
cession crawled down to the village. The widow's
hand pinched Offerton's elbow more tightly than
the occasion required. She had drawn down her
thick veil and her face was almost invisible.

"Ay, poor Ben, he's been took fro' me at last,"
she sighed. "Like grass we be cut down, like
to the flower of the field."

As the dead man was lean and of short stature,
the bearers did not need rest until they reached
the lich-gate. After they had spent some minutes there, the parson came from the rectory
and led the way into the church. There Mrs
Bagshawe and her cousin knelt side by side,
his right leg covered with her voluminous skirt.
Neither gave much thought to the deceased, for
each was dreaming vaguely of the future. At
the graveside, when the sexton flung earth on
the coffin, the widow wept comfortably, as if
relieved of some painful care.

When all was over, the folk hastened to the
Black Bull, all with keen appetites, for a whiff
of the roasted ducks had actually pierced the
dense foliage of the elms and stolen into the
church. At table, Mrs Bagshawe poured out
the tea, plentifully lacing each cup with rum.
Offerton carved the ducks, and in a very short
time all allusion to the dead man ceased. When

the cloth was removed, several bottles of whiskey were brought in, and the guests became noisy.

Mrs Bagshawe rose soon and went to a remote window recess that was screened from the rest of the room by a dingy green curtain. Seeing that Offerton did not venture to follow, she gave several provocative little coughs. At last he rose, unobserved by any of the party, and sat beside her on a low stool.

"O Frank, lad," she said; "yo' dunna know what I've suffert o' late. Et seems such a long time sin' yo' were up at Silver Cliff, an' I've hed a seet to beer! Ben, he couldna stan' th' least crossin', an' on'y a week afore he were called whöam he threw an' owd pewter pot at my yëad, all 'cause I'd browt him small beer 'stead o' Tadcaster. I thowt th' small 'ld be best for him, for I felt as his brain were goin'. Eh dear! eh dear!"

She wiped her eyes and folded the handkerchief on her lap into a neat square.

"Dunna fret, wench," he said, tenderly. "Et were th' will o' God as he should be took. Et were a hard way for a chap to die, an' I've no daaht as yo've bin welly shocked, but et esna th' end o' th' world. Maybe yo'll see things breeter later on. I've heerd o' widow women mekin' up theer minds for another man as soon as the owd un were put away."

Her own tea had not been unlaced: her eyes

were sparkling like beads; there was a pink flush on her smooth, downy cheek, and her parted lips showed two rows of glistening white teeth. She put her moist fingers into his palm and tickled it kindly.

"Ef yo 'll sweer none to let aat to onybody," she whispered, "I'll tell yo' summat?"

"I 'll sweer owt as yo' wish, Em, yo' may trust me. I 've always bin fond o' yo'."

She leaned on his shoulder: her soft, glossy brown hair rubbed against his ear.

"Ben 's left me well-to-do," she said. "I 'm a warmer woman nor I ever thowt to be."

"Yo 're none goin' to say as yo' wunna look on th' same side o' th' road as me!" he exclaimed, excitedly.

She giggled like a young girl. "Hoosh, that esna et. Et 's summat as 'll prove how I care for yo'. . . . Ben were a seet jealous o' yo' bein' my lad afore I wedded him, though he kep' et fro' all save me. Th' very morn as he hanged hissen, he miscalled yo', an' I threaped him down as I fancied yo' a fat lot more nor him. . . . He het me, he did, though nob'dy knows et, an' I dared him to lay a finger on me again; an' after thet he goes out to th' barn.

"He didna coom in when dinner were set, an' I went an' foun' him swingin' wi' his toes wi'in an inch o' th' threshin' floor an' his face twistin' all shapes. An' I thowt et best to let him stop theer. He might hev killed me ef I'd helped him down, for his mind were dazin',—onyhow theer 'ld hev been no peace for as long as he lived, so I just shut th' hatch an' slipped back an' hed my mëat an' went to look again i' hawf-an-hour."

Offerton's face had grown marigold colour.

"Yo' see, I've always fancied yo', Cousin Frank. Ef yo' coort me, well, theer's no knowin' what I may say i' a twelvemonth."

A drunken farmer called her to the table.

"Mrs Bagshawe, mam, wheer are yo'? Coom an' hev yo'r health drunk."

She stole forward and sipped languidly from her glass.

"Health an' prosperity, an' may God send yo' as good a man as Ben."

"Et's undecent to speak o' that," she responded, with a mock-modest smirk. "Let him rest i' his grave. Et esna fit to sug-gest such things at a funeral. Yo' mek me feel rect daan 'shamed!"

Soon afterwards she returned to the window, but Offerton was no longer there. She saw Mrs Fearnehough come in with more bottles of whiskey and she inquired concerning his whereabouts.

"I think th' spirits hes touched him," the landlady said. "He's an abstemious man by nature, but he's badly like just now. I met him at th' door, an' he gev me soom soft talk. He were goin' whöam, for, says he, theer's a devil i' th' parlour. Hee! hee!"

A MAN AND A BROTHER

A MAN AND A BROTHER

A BOW-LEGGED pedlar, with a big white bundle that was shapeless as a rolled-up feather-bed, crawled slowly up the Sir Charles hill. The unwalled track had once been the coach-road between Barlow-St-Anne's and Derby; it was now deep rutted and stony, and only used for traffic by the farmers who bought their lime at the kilns in Milton Dale. The banks were bright with the snowy-flowered clusterberry, whose leaves are like those of the dwarf box; here and there a spring bubbled up into a shallow cresspool. To the west lay the moor, with its broken Druid's Circle; to the east arable land, ruined lead mines, and plantings of wind-tortured firs. North and south nothing was visible save the rigs of the edges, cutting sharply into a hot, white sky.

It was twenty years since the pedlar had climbed that hill. He had given up huckstering in his early manhood, and had become stableman to a poor nobleman in the next county. His master had died some months ago, and being weary of service, he had spent all his savings in the furnishing of a well-stocked pack. He was going on to Great Hucklow, where his folk had lived, to induce such old friends as were left to buy his gaudy dress-pieces and handkerchiefs and sham jewellery.

The sun was setting when he reached the concave of the hill-top. A little brown inn, with a forecourt full of nasturtiums and sweet peas lay a-front a beech copse. On the strip of parched grass before the gate two poles upheld the worn-out signboard of *The Cat and Bells.*

" Et hesna changed a bit," the pedlar said. " Thank th' Lord I 'm here ! Ef on'y they 've gotten soom whöam-brewed like as they used, I 'll be more nor satisfied."

In the forecourt he paused to read the name on the lintel.

" Jason Grayson ! So th' owd lad 's livin' yet ! Et seems as ef th' country hed lain sleepin' e'er sin' I left ! " He mopped his forehead. " By 'r leddy, Sir Charles runs fat aat o' one ! "

He opened the door and went in ; a young girl came from the kitchen.

" Es Jason in ? " he asked, throwing his pack on the broad seat that ran round the tap-room.

" No ; gran'feyther 's gone to Tidsa Fair. He 'll none be back till neet. Mun I draw yo' owt ? "

" Hev yo' ony whöam-brewed ? Ay ; that 's a good job ! Fetch a quart, I 'm main dry."

As he sat to the clean-scoured round table and took his first draught from the pewter tankard another man entered, carrying a camp-stool and an easel. He was thin and ferret-faced, and dressed in a shooting suit of foolish pattern.

"Gin an' wayter," he cried, pompously.

The pedlar rose and went to his side. "I'm blest ef et esna 'Riah Yellot!'" he exclaimed.

The artist eyed him curiously. "I dunna know yo'," he said. Whereat the pedlar held up his swollen right hand, of which the third and fourth fingers were missing.

"Dost rec'lect Gunpaader Day thretty year ago?"

Uriah cackled. "Ef et esna Trestle-Legs Joe!"

"Yo're reet." The pedlar clinked sixpence on the table to pay for the other's drink. "I'll stan' treat. Et's like owd times seein' yo' again. Haa's th' world used yo', Riah?"

"Pretty middlin'. I were forced to gi'e up cobblin' long ago. Fowk mun hev my pictures. I'm welly run off my feet paintin' this an' that. I'm agate o' Demon's Dale just now—look at et."

He held up a muddy umber and pea-green canvas. "Et esna bad for a self-towt chap, es et?" he continued. "An' all these things on th' walls here are mine,—yon chimney sweeper, an' Little Red Riding Hood, an' th' platters o' trout an' game. Ten shillin' a-piece es what I get; but when I'm dëad an' gone, I reckon they'll be wuth theer weight i' gowd. Ef on'y I'd tuk to et younger, I'ld hev bet ony man livin'."

F

Trestle-Legs feigned enthusiastic admiration. In his old master's house there was a fine gallery, and he knew that Elliot's pictures were worse than valueless ; but he was his host, and had been his playfellow.

"An' haa's yo'r brother Job gettin' on ? " he asked, after a short silence.

Uriah frowned sourly. " He went whöam more nor two year ago," he replied.

Just then an under-sized woman, who had been tatting in a side parlour, came to the door. She held a bone shuttle and some thread in her hand. Unseen by either man, she spat furiously in the direction of the artist, and then returned to her seat beside the scarlet geraniums and blue Katy-plants of the window.

" Dear, dear ! " Trestle-Legs said. " I were fond o' him : I can see him naa, just breeched, wi' pretty braan curls, like rock-sticks. He were ten year or more younger nor yo'. Haa did he coom to dee ? "

It was Uriah's favourite story. His face brightened, and he cleared his throat.

" Et were a sad case i' a way," he began, " but theer does seem to be fowk entended by th' Lord to go street to th' devil. When he grew up to a big fellow, he fell to bad ways an' tuk to drinkin'. Mother were livin' then, an' hoo upheld him. I were nowt to her : he'd coom when her thowts o' child-beerin' were ower, an' hoo med a god o' him.

" Then hoo got big wi' dropsy, an' went off
quite sudden, an' 'stead o' what I expected, theer
werna a penny i' th' haase." He lowered his voice.
" An' then I heerd fro' Jason Grayson as Job 'd
gotten his niece into trouble. Whate'er he 'd sin
i' th' wench I canna onderstond, for hoo were th'
fowest on th' country-side. Hoo were red-haired
an' pitted so wi' smallpox yo' couldna lay a pin-
point on a smooth bit o' skin, an' hoo 'd on'y one
eye — t' other 'd bin lost i' th' complaint. By
jowks, hoo were a specimen! Job wanted to
wed, but her feyther were high an' meety (Barlow
win'mill b'longin' to him), an' he put a stop to
et, an' as luck 'ld hev et, th' babby were still-
born. So Job hired hissen to Greaves i' th'
Woodlands, an' I heerd no more o' him for gettin'
on nine year. Jason's niece hes stayed here onct
or twice, but none o' late. Hoo 's enaa to turn
anybody sick to look at."

" An' did Job die wi' Greaves ? " Trestle-Legs
inquired.

" I 'm coomin' to that. No, he didna. He
cem back two year last May, an' med his way
into th' haase just as ef 't were his own. He 'd a
long tale to tell me, but I knew ower well there
werena a word o' et true. Said as haa he 'd bin
a sober man all th' time he 'd bin i' service, an'
haa he were wantin' to start for hissen wi' a bit
o' lond. He 'd saved soom paan's an' theer were
a farm by Greaves's as he 'ld tek. He 'd coom

back for owd time's sake, he reckoned! Th'
wench's feyther were dëad an' he 'd left nowt
worth speakin' o', for the steam-mill at Hassage
'd tuk his trade away, an' naa Job were goin'
to wed her.

"I couldna turn my own flesh an' blood fro'
th' door, for fowk 'ld hev talked, so I med shift
to gie him hawf my bed. We set up till mid-
neet, an' then I went to th' chamber an' stripped
an' fell asleep. Et were daylect when I woke, an'
he werena by my side, so I tip-toed down i' my
shirt, an' saw him sittin' dozin' by th' table, wi'
a bit o' sunleet touchin' th' back o' his yëad.

"His bad days 'd marked him : he were like
a man o' fifty—haggard an' thin an' goin' grey.
Squire Dornton 'd commissioned me for one just
then, so I donned, an' got a jug full o' beer an'
spilt soom ower his vest, an' threw a pack o' owd
cards on th' table an' floor, an' fixed a broken
pipe betwixt his fingers. He were too dog-
weary to wake. Then I gets aat a canvas an'
dashes away till et were doon. Et were th' very
spit o' him, an' et didna tek more nor two hour.
I called et 'Th' Prodigal Son,' an th' Squire gev
me a guinea, an' my word, didna he praise et ?"

Trestle-Legs' lips, which were drawn together
tightly, opened, and he asked, in a sharp voice—

"An' Job—when he woke—what did he
say ?"

"Oh, he just gipped as ef he 'd dropped i'

cowd wayter. Then says he, 'Es et like?'
an' says I, 'Ay,' an' he set his foreyëad on
th' table and began belderin'. An' when that
were ower he cowt howd o' my arm. 'Riah,'
says he, 'ef I'm spent an' broken daan like
thatten, theer's no use i' tryin'.' So I tuk him
to th' glass an' showed him, an' he saw, seem-
ingly for th' first time, haa his sins hed laid
their sign."

"Well," rasped out Trestle-Legs, "how did
he go on then?"

"I'm 'shamed to say. He started drinkin'
again, an' ne'er gev ower for a three-week. I
couldna' do wi' him i' th' haase then, so he stayed
at *Th' Goat.* An' at th' end o' th' three-week
he'd fits an' deed. He were a weak, bad lot,
were Job; rotten to th' core. Et were badness
as killed him."

The woman came out from the parlour and
stood before them. She was red-haired and
pock-marked, and she had only one eye. She
bristled with venom like an angry snake.

"Yo're a blested liar!" she hissed. "Yo'
killed my Job! Yo' broke his heart!"

Trestle-Legs lifted his pack composedly, tak-
ing no further notice of the astonished artist.
At the door he held out his hand to the woman.

"Yo' did reet, missus," he said, fervently.
"I'm glad yo' towd him."

THE LAST POSSET

THE LAST POSSET

THE Yeld is a small, stuccoed farmstead, lying in a concave on the south slope of Milton Edge. Three or four fields surround the buildings; beyond, in every direction, runs the moor with its marshes and rocks and tumuli. A few spruce firs shelter the house from the east wind: the storms of two centuries have made them lop-sided and bent the trunks bow-shape, so that such as are nearest rest their tops on the lichened slates.

Miss Bimble was toiling up the sandy path, with a basket of provisions bought in the village of Milton, which lies out of sight beyond the curve of the valley. There was a look of virtuous resolution on her puckered face, an uncommon kindliness that for the nonce made her almost comely. At the stile, where the path entered the first field, she put down her burden, "phewed," and mopped her forehead with her apron.

"By 'r leddy," she muttered, "et's more nor hot—et's griddlin'. I reckon I suffer more wi' bein' fat. When that poor lad Aitchilees were a-courtin' me, we used for to think nowt o' th' climb—et were but child's play then. But I measured nineteen inch raand th' waist i' those

89

days, an' naa I'm forty an' five inch! Solid flesh, tho'," she struck her bosom heavily with her closed hand; "better nor 's to be fun' naa'-days!"

A cur-dog came limping towards her from the house. She recognised it as belonging to her nearest neighbour, an old farmer who lived two miles farther along the Edge. When she reached the gate of the cobbled yard, where the stable and house front and "shippon" formed three sides of a court, in whose midst steamed a lush, dock-grown manure heap that was surrounded by a brown moat, she saw her visitor sitting on the pig-block beside the door.

"Good e'en to yo', Hannah," he said.

"Good e'en, James. God's mercy, haa I hev sweated!"

"Ay, et 's close. Theer's thun'er abaat. An' yo 've been weighted, too. . . . I thowt I 'ld coom ower wi' a bit o' news for yo'. I went ower th' hill to Thornhill this morn, to see haa Aitchilees Chapman were gettin' on."

She unlocked the door. "Coom in an' hev a sup o' beer," she said. "I tapped et yesternoon—et 's th' March brewin'. Well, an' haa 's he doin'?"

"I 'm sorry to say as he 's dëad—he died just afore I got to th' spot."

"Eh dear! eh dear! an' he were such a fine fellow, he were. An' on'y fifty. Whate'er mun his wife an' childer do? Hoo 's no push abaat her, an' th' eldest gal esna owd enow to go to sarvice!"

"Th' woman as were nursin' him said as he'd begged an' prayed as they shouldna be sent to th' Bastille. Th' wife's abed wi' another babby— th' tenth, an' hoo couldna be wi' him at th' last. Theer's talk already o' gettin' up a 'scription an' fixin' em up i' a shop."

"I'll tell yo' what, James, ef they do I shanna be again gi'in' summat. I've thowt o' helpin' 'em all day. Yo' know fowk said once upon a time as he were after me?"

"Oo, ay, I hevna forgot. Yo' jilted th' poor chap, yo' did."

She bridled foolishly and ran on tiptoe (to show that she was still agile) to the pantry, where she drew a pot of ale.

"I wunna tell yo' what I'll gie," she said. "I might surprise yo'. Theer'll be little need o' other 'scriptions when they get mine. Sup savagely, man, theer's plenty more."

He drained the mug and laid it heavily on the table.

"No more, thank yo', Hannah. Et's good, thatten—none o' malt-coom-an-peep-at-th'-wayter stuff. Naa I mun really go, milkin's near, an' my owd lass 'll be gettin' oneasy."

When he had started, she called her own kine, with a shrill, oily: "Leddy, coom up, coom up, leddy," and milked and set everything

in order for the night. After she had returned
to the house-place; she went to an oaken cabinet
that stood between the hearth and the window.
It was a fine piece of furniture, carved with scenes
from Holy Writ. Here Daniel scowled at man-
faced lions; there Balaam mercilessly flogged his
ass.

She unlocked one of the topmost doors and
took from the shelf an uncouth pitcher of shiny
green ware, covered with monstrous figures in
high relief. As dusk was falling, she lighted a
candle, so that she might watch the glittering of
the bulging sides.

"I dunna like to part wi' et, but et seems my
duty," she said, sadly. "Ets bin i' aar fam'ly for
hunnerds o' years. Feyther always hed et as a
sailor brought et fro' Chaney."

She passed her hand over the rotund belly.

"Mony's th' carouse yo've helped!" she murmured, in fond apostrophe. "Mony's the Bimble
as hes gone to bed wi' een small as grey peas
after suppin' fro' thee. But thaa mun go to save
Aitchilees' bäirns. I'm fain to part wi' thee, but
no paar upon earth 'ld mek' me touch th' money
as I saved as es i' th' bank."

The dragons' eyes winked seducingly, tempting
her to a last posset.

"We'll part i' mirth. Good owd frien's hev
we bin, an' to-morrow I mun tek thee daan to
Squire Bagshawe's, an' mind him as he offered

ten good pun' for thee when he set him daan for
a drink last Twelfth. I little thowt that I 'ld
ever find i' my heart to part wi' thee, but thaa
mun know I were fond o' Aitchilees, tho' I did
gi'e him th' mitten. I were sure as he were
after th' land, an' I 'd heerd as he 'd walked more
nor once wi' th' wench he wed for th' first wife.
. . . He might hev her for me: hoo were fow
as neet!"

She put the jug on the oven-top to heat, and
went again to the pantry, to draw another pint of
ale.

" Feyther said as thaa wert to pass to my eldest
lad," she said, as she returned; "an' as I hevna
ony childer, an' surely ne'er will have ony naa,
et 's as well thaa 'rt goin'. Cousin Richard
Henry 's my heir, an' I wouldna hev his slut o' a
wife chippin' bits aat o' thee, an' belike gi'en thee
to th' childer for a plaything. Nay, thaa 'dst best
go an' set up Aitchilees' young uns for life."

The door of the cabinet still hung open,
showing a row of stone-ware pint bottles.

" Et shall be a posset—a Kirsmas posset i'
harvest time. Little else but posset hes been
drunk aat o' thee i' my livin' mem'ry. An' et
mun be th' strongest posset as thaa 'st held i' thy
belly for mony a long year. Gin i' et, an' rum,
an' whiskey, an' nutmegs, an' cloves, an' ginger.
I wunna hev no milk—a gill o' cream wi' lump
sugar 's th' best. An' a raand o' toast to soften et."

She took a little brass saucepan from the rack and poured in the ale and set it over the clear heart of the fire. One by one she dropped in the spices, and when the contents had begun to simmer, she moved the pan to the hob and cut a slice of bread. This she toasted until it was of uniform straw-colour; then she broke it into the posset jug and soaked it with cream. The ale sent a pungent aroma through the room.

"Et's abaat ready," she said, sniffing. "Naa I mun pour et in. By th' godlings, et smells gran'! I'll do thee honour, owd jug; et's the last posset as e'er I'll sup fro' thee, an' I'll mek et rëal powerful."

She filled a tea-cup with neat rum and added it to the rest, stirring carefully meanwhile. When she believed it to be thoroughly mixed, she used the same quantities of whiskey and gin. The fragrance actually brought tears to her eyes.

"I amna sure as I hevna put too much sperrit to et, but I do consider et's a success. Here's to thy good health i' th' fine place thaa'rt goin' to. Thaa'lt stan' i' a press full o' Crown Derby— better comp'ny thaa'st ne'er known!"

She drank and smacked her lips. "I've fun' aat haa to mek posset naa, I do b'lieve," she exclaimed, gleefully. "I ne'er supped such i' my life afore."

Then she drew the table nearer the settle and snuggled in the warmest corner. "I'll think

abaat Aitchilees as I drink. Happen he'll know
as he's i' my mind, an' as I'm tendin' to do well
for them as he's left behind. Like as not my
help'll set the childer all on theer feet. They
may coom to be well-to-do fowk, an' all aat o' my
posset jug!"

The blood, chilled for so many years, grew
warm and vigorous as she sipped and sipped. The
coarse brush of her fancy painted bright pictures
of the past—vignettes akin to those one sees
on the porcelain faces of old Derbyshire "long-
sleeved clocks." She saw herself leaning on his
arm as they strolled through meadows aglow with
daffy-down-dillies and primroses; she saw him
waiting for her at the "leppings" of the Milton
Brook. Then they were kneeling together in one
of the square pews of the church, praying from
one book. It seemed to her as if she heard his
voice, soft and wheedling as ever.

"Aitchilees, lad, I looved yo', I did," she
whispered.

It was near bedtime now: she took up the jug
and drank what was left with one long gulp.

"I'm afeard et's gotten i' my yead," she
sighed, faintly. "I'm sick-like—I do b'lieve I've
tekken a drop too much!"

She stretched herself full length on the lang-
settle, and fell asleep and dreamed that she was
turned out of the house for debts that she knew
nothing about. When she awoke, candle and fire

were out and the room was in utter darkness. She felt as if she cared not whether she lived or died, but her depression was not caused by her lover's death. Rain was beating loudly against the windows; a rumble of thunder shook the air.

She rose, and with the sudden motion, upset the three-legged table. The posset jug fell to the hearth and broke into fragments.

" Drat th' thing, an' drat et an' drat et!" she snarled. " Aitchilees' brats'll hev nowt fro' me naa!"

And she stumbled blindly to the door.

THE END OF THE WORLD

G

THE END OF THE WORLD

IT was the first night of the Wakes, and the carrier's big cart was crowded with folk who came from the neighbouring country to visit their relations and friends. The greasy lamps that diffused a rank, fishy smell threw quivering lights on fantastic bonnets, that ranged in style from the antiquated scuttle with its fall of black net embroidered with chenille of the rich old farmer's wife, to the saucy tangle of scarlet poppies that crowned the auburn plaits of the innkeeper's daughter.

In the right-hand corner, farthest from the door, sat a withered spinster, dressed in a crape gown and a loose bertha of knitted silk which her mother had worn forty years ago. Her peaked face was very wan, and her eyes sparkled in the semi-darkness like live coals.

The woman who sat nearest to her noted her suppressed excitement, and offered her a draught from a jack-bottle of gin.

"Tek a pull, Miss Bland," she said. "Trouble's owercoomin' yo'. I reckon yo'r brother's end's bin a sad trial."

The spinster waved her uncouthly - gloved hand. "Hoosh!" she whispered, faintly,

99

"they 're talkin' abaat a roary-boary-ailis daan theer!"

The wearer of the scuttle was describing a meteor which she had seen in the night.

"Well, I 'd just wakkened an' turned raand i' bed when a leet 'gan to shine ower th' moor— exactly as ef th' day were breekin'. But I felt as I hedna bin abed long, so I ups an' looks at mester's watch, an' et were on'y five minutes past twelve. 'O Lord,' says I, 'th' heather mun be afire an' th' corn 's ready for cuttin!' Peter he hears me an' slips fro' th' bed an' draws up th' blind, an' when we looks aat, we sees all th' north sky blazin' wi' colours like a rainbow. Et were i' th' form o' a crown at first, then et gethered westwards an' changed to summat like a sword. Theer wcrena hawf-an-hour ere et died, but nayther me nor mester slept a wink after. I 've heerd as et 's a sign o' fair weather."

The girl with the poppies chimed in with: "Fayther said as fowk proffersied th' end o' th' world fro' et!"

A low moan crept from the spinster's lips. She had slept heavily at the house in the distant town where her brother had died, and this was the first she had heard of the apparition. She pressed her thin hands against the back of the seat and attempted to rise, but fell back awkwardly.

" I canna tell 'em," she muttered. " Et 'ld breek their hearts. Best for et to coom like a thief i' th' neet."

The facetious man who sat in the opposite corner overheard her last words.

" Bless me, mam, hes somebody stole yo'r purse?" he said. " Yo' do look bad."

She strove to regain her self-possession.

" No," she replied, with a sickly smile. " Et 's on'y as I 'm more nor a bit tired. I 'll be all reet i' a day or two—ay, me, what am I sayin', when th' world's—I mean when I 'm a' whöam."

" I s'pose yo 'r feelin' duller 'cause o' bein' away fro' yo'r young chap," he remarked, giggling foolishly. " I b'lieve as yo 've never bin parted for so long sin' he began coortin' yo', thirty-five year sin'."

To their credit, the other travellers ignored his attempt to excite their mirth. The story of her courtship belonged to the older generation, and although in her early days folk had spoken jestingly of the lovers who could never make up their minds to wed, time had accustomed them to look compassionately upon the affair. The sole hindrances had been two old mothers who had declared that their homes should never be broken up. But they had died fifteen years ago, and the courtship had continued until both were grey and wrinkled.

The cart lumbered on and on—along the rough heath road that undulated like the waves of a stormy sea—down the steep hill and across the ford of the Derwent, where the waters, swollen with a flood in the uplands, touched the horse's bellies and wet the straw near the door. Then through the long stretch of woodland, and up the Lydgate lane to the village.

Afront the *Bold Rodney* the passengers alighted. A round-shouldered gaffer with a bright, kindly face helped the spinster down the steps and swung her cow-hair trunk over his back.

"Yo're lookin' faint, Sarah," he said, "an' I dunna wonder. Et'ld try yo' sorely bein' wi' him at th' last. By jowks, I hev bin lonesome wi'aat yo'—et seems a year o' Sundays sin' yo' went away. Yo'll soon be rect, tho'. I stepped across to th' house after tea, an' I dusted all an' leeted th' fire an' set th' kettle on, an' then took th' cat an' laid her i' th' chair. Yo'll be ready for yo'r supper?"

She caught his arm, for her knees were giving way.

"I canna eat owt—I shanna want onything else to eat or drink," she groaned. "*O Dave, th' end o' th' world's coomin' to-neet!*"

He gave such a start that the strap of the trunk loosened and it fell heavily to the ground. The intensity of her manner and his knowledge of her truthfulness brought instant conviction.

"An' all them 'ams i' pickle, an' th' owd mare due to foal to-morrow!" he lamented.

"Dunna bother abaat such things," she whimpered. "Theer's weightier matters i' hond. Coom indoors, an' I'll tell yo' all abaat et. Et's no use frightin' other fowk; we mun beer et oursens."

He followed to the house-place and set the trunk on the dresser, and stood tremblingly waiting for her to disburden herself of the fatal news. She untied the strings of her bonnet, and unfastened the glossy buttons of the bertha.

"Et were th' neet after Jake's buryin'," she began, hurriedly. "I'd gone to th' market-place for a change, for th' house were that stiflin', an' I wanted to be whöam again, but Jane said I mun stop another day. An' theer were a man preachin' on th' steps o' th' cross—an aged, venerable man like th' picture o' Is-yah i' th' Bible."

She paused for breath. "An' what did he tell yo'?" Dave stammered.

"He said as he'd med it up aat o' th' proffercies i' th' Owd Testament an' th' Revelations i' th' New as th' world were doomed. But we were to hev a sign gi'en—a breet leet i' th' sky at midnight—a leet sim'lar to th' roary-boary-ailis as cem last neet, an' twenty-four hours after that everything 'ld hap as he foretold. Th' dëad 'll rise. Eh dear! eh dear!"

She began to sob violently; Dave put his arm around her waist.

"Wench," he said, with much fervour, "dunna fret. Yo've done nowt to be 'shamed o', an' no more hev I, an' ef we mun die, well, we mun. Hark to th' kettle boilin'; theer's buttered cake i' th' oven. Surely theer's no call for us to go wi' empty bellies. An' for th' Lord's sake dunna let's mention what's coomin' till we've doon eatin'."

So they partook of a comfortable meal, and when it was finished, Sarah washed the cups and dishes and replaced them on the rack.

"We've on'y got two more hours to live, Dave," she said, quietly. "If I could hev hed my way, I'ld hev chosen soom other time. Th' 'owd-man apples' is finer nor they've bin sin' mother died, an' theer's that bacon o' yo'rs wi' none to eat et."

"Never bother," he said, despondently. "Et'll be all th' same soon. Let us sit an' wait hond-i'-hond."

They drew nearer the hearth and rested silently until the tall clock struck eleven. Then Sarah rose and moved her chair to the wall.

"Lad," she said, "s'pose we go daan to th' churchyard an' wait theer. Yo'r fowk an' mine are buried alongside, an' et'ld seem more respectful ef we were theer when they cem up. I'll tek a shawl to put under us."

. He agreed at once, and they went stealthily down the dark street and over the stile to the south side of the church. There they sat on the grass beside a square tombstone that was embellished with designs of cherubim, and death's-heads, and hour-glasses. As time passed Sarah's head sank to her lover's shoulder. She was worn out with excitement and fatigue. In a few minutes she fell asleep.

Twelve chimed from the tower and Dave was filled with supreme terror. But no thunderclap came, nor did the graves show any signs of subterranean disturbance. He also began to grow drowsy and he leaned back against the stone, his face touching hers.

Dawn broke, a glorious red dawn, and soon the sunlight touched their eyelids. They awoke simultaneously, and after a moment of amazement, Sarah drew herself away, blushing like a young girl.

" That fellow were a liar an' a brute," she cried, angrily, " gettin' two decent fowk to stop aat-o'-doors all neet. Whatever 'll Milton say cf et gets abaat? We mun steal whöam afore onybody 's stirrin'."

When they entered her garden, they heard the whistling of an approaching ploughboy. Sarah tried to run along the narrow path, but stumbled over a projecting currant bough, and Dave was obliged to carry her indoors.

"Ef we've bin seen aar character's gone," she wailed. "Milton were e'er th' evilest thinkin' spot i' th' Peak!"

But her lover only laughed. "I fear theer's nowt for us but to get wed at onct," he said. "Yo' want someone to look efter yo'. I'll go an' tell parson abaat th' spurrin's this morn. An' now I mun go an' see how th' mare's gettin' on."

CUCKOO TIME

CUCKOO TIME

A PATH diverges from the Orgreave turn-pike, just opposite the heather-covered bole, and passes, green and marshy, to the Gadridge Clough, where the peat-stream spreads from the moor edge like a wind-blown grey mare's tail. There the ground becomes sandy and full of pebbles, thridded at intervals with tiny gullies—relics of the wintry storms. The Cuckoo Stones, where the bird of Spring is first heard in Peakland, jut out like platforms from the hill-top. The path crosses them in a warm hollow, then turns abruptly and descends the greater valley of Hollow Dale, where lie the twin farms of Wildeve Spans and Whetstone Lowe.

Jesse Ash hurried through the garden of Wildeve Spans and found the young widow sitting in the porch, knitting a garter and pondering contentedly on the prospects of the next hay season. She was a plump, white-skinned, dark-haired woman with prettily odd features. It was nearly two years since her husband, old Peter Furness, had died, and this year she had relieved the sombreness of her aspect by donning mauve ribbons and a brooch and ring of dull garnets.

Five bachelors were courting her, and she gave a separate evening to each, but reserved Saturday and Sunday for meditations upon the virtues of the defunct spouse. She showed preference to none of her suitors, treating all tantalisingly alike, without the least change of mood. Milton gossip proclaimed her dog-in-the-mangerism, and predicted that she and the men would all come to the churchyard unwed. Besides her charms of person, she possessed a comfortable little fortune, and had expectations of good legacies from divers aged relatives.

Jesse was the youngest of the lot; in fact, he was the widow's senior by only a fortnight. He was a tall, strapping fellow with a brown face, roughly carved as the gargoyles of the church, and a pair of big blue, laughing eyes, and a head of bright golden hair, all crisp and curly. Moreover, he had a sharp wit, which the widow, although half afraid, was wont to excite with tantalisingly silly remarks.

His farm, Whetstone Lowe, was on the farther side of Hollow Dale, and the sharp walk had brought beads of perspiration to his forehead. Mrs Furness watched them gather together and fall, with audible splashes, on the freshly sanded floor.

"I'll tell yo' what, Jesse," she said, kindly. "Yo'll sweat yo'rsen till theer's nowt left!

An' yo're thin as a grewhaand already! Sit yo' daan; I'll get you a mug o' ale."

"Ay, et's hot weather, hot weather for th' time o' th' year. Et's gran' th' way yo'r whöats es coomin' up."

She bustled away to the house-place where an elderly woman was gophering things with dainty white frills. In a side kitchen the men-servants were smoking lustily.

"Will yo' go to th' cellar, Anne," said the widow, "(I've gotten on my thin slippers) an' draw a pint o th' best for Mester Ash. He's coom a bit afore his time."

Anne chuckled meaningly. "Ay, I'll go," she replied, as she moved to the pot-rack. "Deary me, I'll draw et clear for him, for he's th' best o' th' gang, he es!"

Mrs Furness took the creaming lustre-ware mug and set it on the seat beside Jesse. He raised it almost to his lips, but paused, bethinking himself of an old-fashioned custom.

"D'yo' sup first, Mrs Furness, an' then et'll be sweeter to th' taste."

She obeyed, blushing faintly. "Oh, yo' men, yo' flatterers," she said, wiping her lips on her handkerchief. "Yo' that can wheedle an' twist a young wench raand yo'r fingers like a thread o' silk! I were silly enow onct mysen—a mony, mony year ago."

"None so mony, nayther," Jesse responded.

"I mind yo' afore yo' wedded Peter. But I were on'y eighteen then—a lad aside o' yo', for a woman gets sense afore a man."

"Ay, I hevna forgot. Yo' stuck burrs i' my hair when I went to get confirmed, an' the owd bishop got his hand's prittled. My word, but he were angry : he towd parson, an' parson grum'led for an hour !"

Then both laughed boisterously, and as twilight was falling they went indoors and sat talking before the fire, whilst Anne continued her ironing of fragrant raiment. Jesse had never found the widow so placable before, and he strove to take advantage of the opportunity to press his suit ; but she shrugged her shoulders and arched her brows so meaningly that his heart sank like a leaden plummet.

When the ironing was finished, Anne laid the table for supper, and the three ate and drank together. Afterwards the woman removed the pots to the kitchen, and Jesse and Mrs Furness drew again to the hearth and gazed into the fire as if they might discover there some subject for conversation.

Jesse broke the silence at last.

"I heerd 'cuckoo' this morn," he remarked.

The widow brightened up wonderfully.

"'Then et 's time for me to think o' choosin' a man," she said.

He moved his chair nearer, and tried to

take her hand, but she hid it under her muslin apron.

"Et es time," he said, with much fervour. "An' I do hope an' pray as yo'll choose me."

She shook her head almost petulantly.

"Et doesna go by ordin'ry pickin' i' our fam'ly," she replied. "Et's luck as does et wi' th' Lees women."

"How's that?" Jesse inquired. "I never heerd o' et."

"Well, ef theer's more nor one chap a-coortin' a wench, the first time as hoo hears 'cuckoo' an' runs to a bank an' sits her daan an' doffs her shoon, hoo'll find a hair or two o' th' one hoo mun marry on her stockin'. Mother towd me— an' i' my own time I found one o' Peter's theer, an' I knew theer were nowt for et but a yes."

"Et'ld be a white un, Peter's," Jesse said, bitterly.

Mrs Furness sighed.

"Ay, he were gettin' on, an' he'd bin wed three times afore; but he were a good man—as good a man as e'er breathed! An' mother were set on him; hoo seemed to know as he'd mek a good husband, for hoo said I mun be thankful as th' sign were given. He were took wi' a ströake first Christmas afterwards, an' as patient as Job for th' rest o' his days."

She wiped her eyes.

"Did yo' e'er see such a corpse, Jesse? White

as a lily, an' tho' et were hot weather, none
workin' i' th' least. I can see him now. Eh
dear, eh dear, he were more like a fayther nor
a husband, he were!"

Soon afterwards Jesse rose to depart. Mrs
Furness went with him to the door.

"Lord help us, et's rainin' now, an' as black
as pitch!" she exclaimed. "Yo' mun hev' a
lantern. Anne, just leet th' owd one an' show
Mester Ash to th' bottom o' th' garden. Them
steps es slipp'ry as fat! I hope et'll be fine
i' th' morn, for I promised to go over to sister
Cockerel's. Good neet, Jesse, lad, good neet."

Anne accompanied him to the wicket. Mrs
Furness retired to the house-place. The farmer's
cheeks were hot, and the light of the candle was
reflected in his sparkling eyes. He took the
candle, but seemed loth to go; and when the
woman turned he laid his hand on her arm.

"Just a moment, Anne, wench. I'll give yo'
a ten-shillin' piece ef yo'll lend me missus's
stockin's an' a needle after hoo's gone to
bed."

She drew back, grinning.

"Yo've gone mad, I reckon. Whate'er d' yo'
want 'em for."

"I wunna tell. On'y coom daan to me i' th'
barn wi' th' stockin's i' an hour, an' I'll put th'
money i' yo'r pawm."

"All reet, Mester Ash. Yo're up to soom

roguery, but I 'll do et. I s'pose yo' dunna want her to know ?"

"Cert'nly not. Yo 're a good soul, Anne, an' yo 'll be no sufferer i' th' future. I 'll just sit wi' th' lantern i' th' pickin'-hole."

She went away and returned before long with a pair of long grey stockings and a needle. Jesse eyed her very shyly.

"Ef yo 'll turn yo'r back I 'll do et better," he explained. "Yo' arena to know owt abaat et."

"Yo' mun be quick, Mester Ash. Hoo esna asleep yet, an' ef hoo got aware as I were aat theer 'ld be soom stirrin's."

She moved aside, and Jesse pulled long hairs from his head and darned them into the insteps of both stockings. Then he gave them to Anne, with instructions to replace them in the widow's chamber, and thanked her, and presented her with double the sum he had promised. The candle was guttering by this time, so he extinguished it, and swaggered home through the darkness, singing foolish old ballads, whose themes were of strategy for women's love.

Early next morning he met Mrs Furness on the path near the Cuckoo Stones. The bird had been calling for the last half-hour—his song evoked by the bright sunshine that had followed the night's rain. The widow was blushing vividly. Her skirts were wet : it was evident that she had been sitting on the grass.

"Good mornin' to yo', Mrs Furness," he said. "Yo 'll hev a gran' walk."

Her gaze was downcast.

"I 'm none so sure as I 'll go," she faltered. "I 've hed a kind o' shock."

"Lord! Nob'dy 's scared yo', I do hope? On'y let me catch him! I 'll breek every böan i' his body!"

"Et esna that, Jesse, et 's a happy shock."

"Yo 're none goin' to be wed?" he cried, in well-feigned complaint.

"I 'm — I 'm p'raps. Jesse, yo 've asked me more nor onct. When I heerd 'cuckoo,' I set me daan an' doffed my shoon, an' fun' my stockin's full o' yo'r hair! Et 's fate, I do b'lieve."

"Et es, an' domned good fate, too, I call et. Gi'e me a kuss."

SACRED AND SECULAR

SACRED AND SECULAR

THE twins had been blind from birth. Their home was a small cottage near the gate of the elm avenue that runs from the Derwent bank, up the hillside to that ancient baronial hall which is known to the tourist as "The Stronghold of the Peak." It was the custom of John, the brother, to wheel out a portable harmonium whenever a waggonette approached from the station, so that he might be heard singing placidly from the book of American hymns that is most popular in that part of the world. A round tin box for the reception of gratuities lay on the ground at his feet, and he was never so rapt in his music as to omit nods of thanks for the downfall of coins. On special occasions his sister Elizabeth, standing beside with folded hands, warbled a treble in a rich soprano that the passage of fifty years had worn but little.

It was their cleanliness and their calm superiority to a common misfortune that inspired Mrs Millwort of the *Swan Tavern* at Milton, who had driven over with a party of friends, to engage them for the next Wakes. She had only occupied the inn for some months,

and was still strange to the profession, her
deceased husband having been a local preacher
in the Woodlands.

"Et 'll raise th' tone," she said.   "Theer's
more mëat i' 'Sweepin' thro' th' Gates' an'
'Will yo' meet me at th' Fountain' nor i' a
thaasand o' 'Jack Jones's.'   All th' good-lived
fowk i' the plaace 'll coom to hear 'em.   Theer
es soom i' Milton, so I 've heerd, as wunna
patronise th' publics at fëast times, just cause o'
th' naughty songs as es sung.   My plaace 'll be
different.   I 'm sure poor Walter 'ld hev done
likewise ef on'y he hadna been took away wi'
quinansies."

So on the first evening of the Wakes the blind
singers arrived in the inn dogcart, sitting on the
back seat with the little harmonium held tightly
between them, and bearing on their laps a
change of raiment done up by a friendly
neighbour in scarlet cotton handkerchiefs.
They were decently dressed, and their faces
beamed with the prospect of a week of good
living and excitement.   There was nothing unpleasant in their aspect; their eyes being in
nowise clouded, and the absence of distressing
outlook on the world had kept their brows free
from wrinkles.   Mrs Millwort met them at the
door and led them in triumph to her private
parlour, conscious of her own good taste in the
choice of such refined entertainers.

" Yo 'll hev tea now," she said, kindly. " I hed
et set, for I knew as yo 'ld be welly tired wi'
fifteen mile o' hard, dusty röad.   An' a nip o'
brown cream for böath, I reckon ? "

" Ay, for me," Elizabeth replied.   " John 'll
tek no tea — he fancies ' Paddy's eye-watter '
best."

" An' he shall hev et," Mrs Millwort said, with
enthusiasm.   " Sarah "—she addressed the girl
in the tap-room — " twopenn'orth o' gin naa,
please."

They ate and drank together, discussing meanwhile a programme for the night's entertainment.

" We hevna a dancin' chamber," explained the
hostess, " an' even if we hed, I 'ld hev' no
dauncin', bein' as et 's again' my principles.
Yo 'll sing i' th' club-room.   I 'ld recommend
yo' to begin wi' hymns wi' a waultsy 'compani-
ment, so as fowk can join in th' chorus.   An'
at th' end o' ev'ry hour yo' can go raand wi'
th' box an' gether in what fowk fancy to give
yo'. . . . Now, mind yo' sing nowt as 'll set 'em
again beer an' spirits.   Theer 's a plea i' th'
Bible for 'em as theer es for owt else."

The singers promised, and an hour afterwards,
at the edge of dark, they were conducted upstairs
to the big chamber with the bow window, where
all the seats were crowded with expectant
frequenters of the inn.   Mrs Millwort intro-
duced her stars with much ceremony.

"Gentlemen an' ladies," she said, "I've gotten two gran' singers, at very greet expense" (four shillings a day was the sum), "an' I trust yo'll do me th' honour o' 'preciatin' 'em. I dunna howd wi' publicans as b'lieves theer's more to be 'tracted wi' a low song than wi' summat genteel an' extraordin'ry. Poor an' dark they be, but clëan an' respectable, an' on'y wantin' to mek an honest livin'."

John sat before the instrument and played the *Hallelujah Chorus*, which feat, being the first, was received with some acclamation. The *March from Judas Maccabæus* followed, and the interest lessened considerably. The solemnity seemed to prevent the audience from sending for fresh glasses, and Mrs Millwort felt a slight pang of dread.

"Sing now, loove," she whispered to Elizabeth; "summat wi' a swing as they can tek up."

In another moment the clear soprano and tenor (they were really excellent in their untrained way) rose in a well-known camp meeting tune. But one by one the mouths of the listeners fell, and a few of the younger sort edged towards the door.

At the end of the first verse, Elizabeth raised her hand. "Join en th' chorus, gents," she said.

Only three or four responded, and these sang in such a spiritless way that a cold perspiration

trickled from the hostess' brow.   When the hymn
was finished, an elderly farmer rose and protested.

"I didna know we were goin' to howd a prayer
meetin', missus," he said, severely.   "Theer's
things i' season an' things aat o' season, an'
hymns at Wakes time es among th' last.   I'm
goin', ma'am, an' I wish yo' a very good neet."

Mrs Millwort clutched John's arm wildly.
"Et's yo' as esna puttin' fire enow en't," she
snapped.   "Play as ef yo'd gotten soom blood i'
yo'r veins."

Again they essayed, but ere the second verse
was finished there were only ten people left in
the room.   The hostess bristled like an angry
hedgehog.

"Ef yo're none goin' to 'tract fowk, et's a
grëat misfortun' as I browt yo'!" she cried.   "I
did et i' charity.   I wish to—I wish I'd got a
punch an' judy show or a juggler instead!   Do
better or back whöam yo' go this very neet!"

"We'll none go whöam wi'aat aar money,
mam," John said, excitedly.   "Six days at four
shillin' a day.   We'll do what we can to earn et,
but we wunna be put upon."

A panic took possession of Mrs Millwort, and
she became as one possessed of seven devils.   The
audience, fearful that she might do some mischief
to her blind artistes, drew her aside to quieten
her, whilst John and Elizabeth talked together in
broken tones.

"We mun do summat, loove," he said. "Th' missus were well disposed to us, an' et's on'y nat'ral as hoo feels bad. But we 've coom to addle our money, an' we 'll hev et. D' yo' happen to remember soom o' those owd songs as feyther used to sing when he were fresh?"

The poor woman blushed. "Ay, John," she replied. "I 'm none ever like to forget 'em. Et 's thretty year sin' he died, an' I 've tried never to think o' em. Yo' know as well as onybody as they were brazzen."

"Well, never mind, sing 'em. We 'll give her a chanct. I can play th' tunes well enow. What d' yo' say to 'Sally, will yo' marry me?'"

"As yo' will, but I munna be bläämed. I 'll on'y do et to save the credit here. Onybody 'll know as I 'm innocent, being' dark."

John coughed in a shrill suggestive way that sounded in Mrs Millwort's ears like the clarion of an angel. She hastened to his side; at his proposal the greyness left her face.

"I see, I see, an' I reckon et a good notion," she said. "Onyhow, I 'm desp'rate, an' we 'll try et. Hoo mun hev' action, hoo mun move abaat as hoo thinks fit. See, I 'll oppen th' window, an' hoo can stan' theer an' sing aat. None stand like a stuffed mummy, ayther, but like a woman. I 'll set a can'le on each side, so as th' fowk on th' green may see all theer es to see."

Out-of-doors the air was a-quiver with the
noise of merry-making. One after another the
gaffers shot for drinks in the gallery. The music
of Mallet's World-Famed Roundabouts was faint
enough ;—fortunately the machine was fixed in a
field behind the church—but ever and anon the
shrill whistle drowned every other sound.

Mrs Millwort flung open the casement, and
Elizabeth moved forward and began to sing.
Whether it was because of her recollections of a
not unhappy girlhood, or because of her con-
sciousness that the prosperity of the inn was at
stake, her voice grew supremely full and piercing,
and her manner so suggestive that the most
advanced music-hall singer might have wondered
and learned. At first people watched and listened
in bewilderment ; it was so unlike anything they
had ever known. After the first pause, however,
and before she sang "The Maid and the Golden
Squire," a crowd swarmed up the staircase and
entered the chamber.

Thus the festival degenerated into an orgie.
The elderly blind woman with the saintly face
and the seraph's voice was transformed into a
bacchante. As she sang her eyes sparkled, and
a mischievous smile wreathed her lips.

Mrs Millwort's relief was so great that she
renounced for ever her intention of raising the
tone of Milton.

"Dom—bless yo' !" she said, as she put a glass

of gin in Elizabeth's outstretched hand, and gave
her a hearty kiss. "Yo 're a success, yo' are. I
hev ne'er heerd such! Lord knows haa yo' got
howd o' such things, but yo' mek 'em coom up
afore aar een. Put me daan for th' next holiday ;
—yo 'll mek a fortune at Wakes times every-
wheer ! . . . Now, loove, they 're askin' for ' Th'
Owd Apron.' "

THE CELEBRITY OF MISS
WHITTINGHAM

THE CELEBRITY OF MISS WHITTINGHAM

I T was after my return from town that I heard
the story. The adventure had happened
on Midsummer Night, and although nine days
had elapsed, Milton still rang with praises of
its heroine. When Miss Elizabeth Whittingham
sent for me, I congratulated myself that I should
only hear an abridged version of the affair, but I
had not taken into account the fact that a tale,
repeatedly told by an old lady, is altogether unlike the rolling stone.

After Job Wilkins the carrier had delivered
her message, and informed me that everybody in
the neighbourhood had visited her, from the old
captain at the Dower House to the curate's wife
from Hassage, five miles away, and that the
doctor had lent her the identical willow-pattern
invalid's cup from which the last Countess of
Newburgh had imbibed beef-tea, I left my eyrie
on the hill-top, and descending to Milton, reached
the cottage where Miss Whittingham dwelt.

One of her spinster friends met me in the
house-place, where I had expected to find the
mistress enthroned in state. In answer to my

inquiry as to whether Miss Whittingham were at home, she raised her brows angrily.

"I should think hoo is a' whöam," she said. "Why, hoo's got th' rheumatics that bad i' her knee as hoo wunna be aat o' bed this sennight. Yo' munna think 'cause a woman's brave, hoo's med o' iron!"

She led me to the kitchen, from whose midst a narrow staircase with balustrades of polished oak rose to the upper floor. Ascending this, the woman tapped at a closed door, and a piping voice cried "Come in." She turned the knob and I entered the old maid's chamber.

The first thing that I saw was the low, latticed window, with a row of windfall cherries lying on the sill, ripening in the hot sunlight. My heart sank as I remembered how she had thrust such fruit upon me in former seasons.

"Et's th' gentlemen fro' th' Edge," the nurse announced. "He actually werena 'ware as yo' were bedfast!"

She disappeared, and I turned respectfully towards the big four-post bed, which was hung with white dimity enlivened with a border of robinets and holly-leaves. The heroine sat up against the plump pillows, gorgeous in a nightcap of mauve wool with green ribbons, and a scarlet cloth dressing-jacket, whose lappets were ostentatiously thrown back, so that the glistening silk lining might be seen. The antique furniture, the odd colouring against the snowy background, and the brown, wrinkled face,—more like a dry winter apple than any other thing,—made a strangely suggestive picture. I might have been in the state-chamber of some old-time cardinal.

Miss Whittingham smiled cordially, disclosing a fine set of teeth, yellow, but not decayed.

"I wanted yo' to coom, mester," she said, "for I like to hev' a chat wi' yo', an' I thowt et would be best for me to give yo' all th' details o' th' affair mysen, for fowk do exaggerate so. What d' yo' think?—my cousin Rafe at Buxton—he's a powtry shop theer—well, he writes sayin' as he'd heerd I'd been het by a lion! But, thank God, et werena so bad as that."

I feigned great interest, and strove to draw her to the subject; but the luxury of a fresh visitor was too overpowering.

"Them cherries in the window-bottom's for yo'," she remarked. "Theer's a quarter o' a paand: I picked 'em up th' mornin' afore et happed. Yo'd three-quarters last summer an' yo' forgot to pay for 'em, an' when yo've tuk this lot et'll be sixpennorth."

I laid the coin on the bed. She took it up, putting on her spectacles to see if the stamp were overmuch worn, then she dropped it into a wash-leather bag that she kept under the bolster. Again I strove to make her speak of the adventure, but instead she treated me with the history

of her several courtships.   I heard once more how
Nathan Yellot of Crosslow had gone to America
because she would not favour his suit; how Dick
Basker, "him wi' th' frog-mark on his cheek,"
had taken to drinking on her account; and how
in later years old Charles Pursglove had sat
with her until midnight, when she suggested his
departure by donning her nightcap.

It was not until I drew out my watch and
declared that I must return that she began the
story of how she had become enrolled amongst
the Brave Folk of Milton.

"Happen yo' didna know afore yo' went to
foreign parts as theer were a wild-beast-show
comin'?   Well, et were billed over th' village for
Friday was a week.   I'd never seen such, though
I've gotten Oliver Gowdsmith's 'Animated
Natyure' among my books; an' theer's pictures
o' Adam namin' th' animals, an Daniel wi' th'
lions, an' Lisha callin' th' she-bears i' th' big Bible.

"Everybody were goin', farmers an' theer wives,
cobblers, shop-folk an' all, an' somehow I didna
care to stop a' whoam.   Th' bills said as gentry
mun pay a shillin', an' workin'-classes sixpence, so,
as I've gotten a bit o' money, 1 med up my mind
to go as a lady."

Suddenly she bethought herself of business.

"Yo're a writin' chap, an' I understand yo' get
money wi't.   If yo' tell 'baat my adventure, I
mun hev hawf."

I consented and she went on with her tale.

"I' th' afternoon, I donned my black bombazeen —et hed bin mother's—bowt for fayther's aunt's funeral—her as died Taddington Wakes."

Here she interpolated a prolix account of her great aunt's will, and of the difficulty her father had in getting possession of his legacy. Despite my endeavours, half-an-hour passed before her own story was resumed.

"I took aat my bonnet wi' bugles an' violets an' my whalebone umbrella—theer's nowt like whalebone; it doesna rust—an' I started off an' paid my shillin' at th' door.

"Eh dear, ef I'd on'y known, I wouldna' hev gone a foot. Th' lions they roared like devils, an' th' snakes were just what fayther declared he saw after a week o' suppin'! An' theer were a dauncin' beer,—a greet foul thing wi' a muzzle like a mad dog. Phew, they all smelt that bad I hevna got th' whiff aat o' my nose yet. Respectin' th' monkeys, th' less said abaat 'em th' better! They're undecent. I cem away th' moment I'd seen everything; for I thowt et werena worth while stoppin'. An' on my way back, I met wi' Lucy Andrews, an' hoo would hev me go on wi' her to tea, an' what wi' talkin' abaat th' beasts, an' what wi' eatin' an' drinkin', et were ten o'clock afore I got whöam.

"Well, I set me down an' took off my mantle an' my bonnet, an' were toastin' my feet on th'

fender (I'd left a turf on an' et were glowin'
well), when I heerd a noise i' th' back garden,
an' med sure one o' Robi'son's lads 'd gotten
at my fayberries again.   They're worse nor
monkeys!

"So I whips up a stick an' unlocks th' door,
turnin' th' key after me an' puttin' et i' my
pocket, for them lads 'ld none be again runnin'
thro' th' house; an' I crawls, mum's a mouse,
up th' steps to th' rhububb bed.   An' theer I
stan's up an' shaats aat: 'I've cowt yo' at last,'
an' Lord hev mercy, et werena a boy, but th' big
braan beer fro' th' wild-beast-show, dauncin' up
an' daan among the fayberry bushes. . . . Yo'll
be sorry to know as I canna sell yo' ony fayberries this summer; but just peep thro' the
window."

I looked out and saw the trampled soil covered
with ancient, green-lichened gooseberry boughs,
and I gave thanks silently, because I was saved
the sour dwarfish fruit.

"I tries to get aat o' seet, but th' beer cooms
close, an' I runs an' thinks how to get away, tho'
th' walls 're tipped with bottle-sherds.   Robi'son's
lads dunna mind that, tho'.   So th' beast begins
followin' me, an' for five minutes I scuttled abaat
as fast as e'er I could.   An' at last I gets near th'
cherry tree, an' God gev me strength to scrawm
up.   Just look again,—th' trunk's eight feet or
more wi'aat a branch!   Parson says et were a

mira-culous thing i' a woman o' seventy. I dunna
rec'lect how I managed, but somehow I got quite
to th' top an' sits me daan i' a fork.

"Then th' brute he begins to climb after me,
but I just brobbed him i' th' eye wi' my stick, an'
he fell back an' polkaed raan' an' raan' till I were
welly dizzy wi' watchin' him. Et were fearsome
to hear him growl. He strove to get up again as
th' church clock were strikin' twelve, but I gev
him another brob an' he were satisfied. After
that he went tramplin' o'er my fayberry trees till
they were as yo' see 'em.

"I did keep screetin', but nob'dy heerd. I felt
as I mun hev bin ten year up that tree, th' time
seemed so long. I were well-nigh done up by
daylight, but one o' Robi'son's lads cem to get
ower the wall, an' gev a great yell when he saw
what were amiss.

"After that I hadna long to wait, for three
wild-beast-showmen who 'd been aat seekin' all
neet cem an' nabbed th' brute, an' muzzled him
an' took him away. Robi'son lifted me daan. I
were that weak I thowt I mun die, an' the owd
rheumatics cem back to my knees.

"Ay, fowk hev bin very good wi' me. Th'
gentleman as th' show belongs to says he 'll hev
th' garden set afresh, an' his wife 's gi'en me a
dress-piece o' silk an' this fine bed-jacket. Everybody 's med me presents, an' th' doctor says I mun
hev plenty o' owd port wine—none clarrit.

"Mun yo' rëally go? Well, good afternoon. What's this? Nay, I didna want owt. Thank yo' very much. Tek them cherries; I've stitched a bag o' blue sugar paper to howd 'em. Et's on th' dressin' chest, under th' hair-brush mat."

A WITCH IN THE PEAK

A WITCH IN THE PEAK

IT was the evening after old Johnny White's funeral, and Elizabeth sat by the low fire in the house-place, wondering how she could manage to exist for the remainder of her days without him who had never spent a whole day apart from her since their wedding, fifty years ago. The bitterness of her spirit was increased by the knowledge that at the end of the week the little farm must be sold to pay the money which the dead man had owed for standing surety for a dishonest cousin. The original sum had been thirty-five pounds; but the lender, Luke Flint, a shoemaker, who was known as "the Milton Spider," from his knack of wrapping a web about such unwary folk as craved aid from him, had stipulated on an interest of fifty per cent. until all was repaid. This interest had eaten up all the profits of the stony acres, and Johnny had died heart-broken because one year's payment was in arrears.

Elizabeth had dismissed all her neighbours. She desired to be left in solitude for such short time as she remained in the house, so that she might recall scenes of bygone happiness. She was quite alone in the world, so that there was

none save herself to suffer ; but still the outlook
was so depressing that the source of her tears was
dried.

"I can see yo' again, Johnny lad," she murmured, "walkin' wi' me fro' church on aar
weddin' morn, as coomly a man as were i' th'
whöal Peak. . . . But yo' looked just as coomly
i' yo'r shroud, wi' all ets pratty gimpings, tho'
yo'r cheeks hed lost theer red, and yo'r gowd hair
were gone as white as snow. Ay lad, ay lad, I
do wish I might hev gone wi' yo' ! When I think
o' all our good life together ; how yo' thowt nowt
were too han'some for me, an' as whate'er I did
were th' reet thing, I'm like to go mad. An'
now I'm to be turned aat o' th' place wheer aar
wedlock's bin spent! Et's hard, et's very
hard ! "

As she lamented, the latch of the door was
lifted and the creditor entered. He was a dark,
squat man of middle-age, with a bullet-shaped
head and blue, close-shaven jowls. His arms and
legs were unnaturally long, and his broad shoulders
were so much bent as to suggest deformity. He
strode forward to the hearth, and without invita-
tion plumped down in the arm-chair which Johnny
had always used.

Elizabeth rose in excessive anger. Her thin
face flushed crimson, her toothless lower jaw
moved oddly from side to side.

"I'll thank yo' to get aat o' that ! " she cried.

" Et 's always bin set in by a honest fellow, an' I
canna see ony other sort use et! Ef yo' mun sit,
sit on th' sattle."

He assumed an air of bravado; but her aspect
was so threatening that he rose sullenly and took
the corner to which she pointed.

"Yo' needna be so haughty, 'Lizbeth White,"
he said, with an unpleasant sneer. "This spot'll
be mine soon, for I 'm agoin' to buy et, an' happen
yo 'll coom a-beggin' to th' door."

" I 'ld liefer starve nor beg o' yo'. What d' yo'
want, a-coomin' rattin'?"

" I on'y want to mind yo' as yo' mun tek none
o' th' things aat o' th' place. My papers 'low me
to sell all, an' if yo' touch owt—off yo' go to
Derby."

She cracked her fingers in his face. " I 'll be
more nor thankful to get aat o' yo'r debt," she
said. " Et 's yo'r cheatin' simple lads like my
John as keeps yo' alive. Yo 're none fit to be
'mongst decent livers. I do b'lieve as th' law
wouldna favour yo'."

His sallow skin grew white and then purple.

" Yo' try th' law, 'Lizbeth White, an' yo 'll find
as et canna touch me. Yo'r man signed th'
agreement to pay me my money, an' ef he
couldna pay et, I were to be at lib'ty to sell
th' lond. Th' lond, say I?—et esna lond—nowt
but three akkers o' stone an' moss, wi'aat a real
blade o' grass! Et wunna fetch thretty pun', an'

I 'm certain sure as th' furniture esna worth ten.
Yo 'll still be soom pun's i' my debt.   I reckon
yo 'll hev to go to th' Bastille, an' I may mek' up
my mind to losin' some o' th' good money ! "

" I 'd go to th' Bastille forty times ower, sooner
nor be behowden to yo' for owt.   But as long as
I 'm stoppin' i' th' haase, I wunna stond yo'r jaw '
Aat yo' go, yo' brute yo' ! "

She unfastened the door, and held it wide open.
It was a dark night, and the air was heavy with
the scent of withered leaves.   The prattle of the
spring as it leaped from the moor-edge to the
trough in the paddock was distinctly audible.

" Yo' owd wretch ! " he muttered.   " I 'll see
as yo' suffer for yo'r brazzenness.   Yo' beggar !
When yo'r a-hoein' taturs i' th' Bastille garden,
I 'll set th' others laughin' at yo'."

He moved leisurely across the floor ; she
sharpened his gait by picking up a besom-
stale.

" Whiles I 'm mistress here, I 'll hev none o'
yo'.   John 's paid yo' time an' time again.   Be
off, yo' skin-a-louse !   I beg an' pray God to
punish yo' this very neet.   Ef et hedna bin for
yo' theer 'ld hev been no buryin' here for mony
a year.   I 'm none one as es gi'en to cursin', but
yo' deserve whatten yo 'll get."

He slunk out into the darkness.   She closed
the door and bolted it carefully, and when the
clatter of his footsteps had died away, she returned

to the chair by the hearth, where a choir of crickets was now singing cheerfully, and delivered herself to the melancholy satisfaction of meditating on past joy and present sorrow.

Meanwhile the Spider walked down the lane in some trepidation, for her violence had unnerved him strangely.

"I do b'lieve hoo's rëally a witch," he said. "Her eyes brenned that red! Ef hoo'd lived i' my greet gran'feyther's days hoo'ld hev bin faggotted, sure enow!"

His mumbling was suddenly cut short by some terrible thing catching the hinder-part of his waistband and plucking him up from the ground. When he recovered his senses in some measure he was on a level with the tree-tops. His voice rose in a harsh shriek.

"Help! All o' yo' help! Jack-wi'-th'-Iron-Teeth's gotten howd o' me an's draggin' me to Hell!"

But as it was late, and the Milton folk were abed, none heard. He flew swiftly through the air, his long arms and legs sprawling frog-like. Once he caught hold of the thatch of a barn and clung for a moment, but the rotten wisps came away in his hands. He gave himself up for lost. The demon was dragging him over the moor in the direction of the river.

"O Lord, forgi'e me, forgi'e me, an' I'll tek' advantage o' innocent fowk no more. I'll do my best to set things reet as I 've set wrong, ef only Thou 'lt let me off this time !' "

He fell with a heavy splash into the marsh of the Wet Withins. For a long time he lay, half-swooning, on a tussock of bent-grass. Then, when his strength returned, he crawled blindly over the heath to the road.

Instead of making for home, he went straight to Crosslow Farm and knocked feebly at the door. Elizabeth was sleeping in her chair. She had been dreaming blithely of years of good crops. She rose, drowsily, and drew back the bolts. In the dim firelight she looked more like a witch than ever.

" Yo 've coom back again !" she said, sharply. " Be off! I wunna hev et said as I let yo' in at this time o' neet !' "

He was trembling like a paralytic.

" Gie me a bit o' paper, 'Lizbeth White," he stammered, " an' I 'll write a quittance. Yo 're a wicked woman, an' I 'll hev nowt more to do wi' yo'. Yo 're on'y fit to bren !"

" I reckon et 's conscience," she said, as she took paper and pen and ink from the corner cupboard. " Write whatever yo' like an' go to ——.' "

" Dunna say thatten, for Lord's sake !" he yelled.

He took the paper and wrote :—" I, *Luke Flint, do hereby forgive Elizabeth White her husband's debt as she owed me, and I trust as she will bear no further malice."*

Then he hastened from the place, as though it held a creature accursed.

Two days afterwards he returned to Crosslow, in a cajoling, lachrymose humour.

"Gi'e me that quittance back again," he said, with a painful giggle. "Yo're an honest woman, I reckon. I thowt yo' were a witch, but et were a b'loon hook as picked me up an' carried me to th' wayter-holes. Soom chaps droppin' advertyse-ments for gin an' whisky 'ld gone astray an' were tryin' to fix on a spot. Summat hed gone wrong wi' th' machine. Gi'e me et back, wench, yo're a reet-dealin' woman, an' I'm sure yo' wunna do but whatten's just."

She laid hold of the besom-stale again.

"I'll breek yo'r back ef yo' dunna go," she cried. "Yo' thowt I were a witch, but yo' munna think I'm a fool!"

MARKET-MERRY

MARKET-MERRY

THE rain had ceased at twilight, and in the gleam of a thin crescent moon the wet limestone roads that crossed the valley shone like flooded rivers. An endless prattling of rillocks that gushed down the hillside drowned every other sound — even the ringing of Milton curfew was scarce heard beyond the confines of the village, although on fine evenings it reached the little town of Tedstone, which lies five miles away, on the east bank of the Derwent.

There was a heavy scent of decaying leaves in the air; now and then the water from the uplands added a pungent whiff of peat. The half-naked elms that ran in two irregular lines from Yeld Farm to the turnpike were occupied by a colony of owls, whose more gamesome members lurched from tree to tree like pillows thrown in a goblin school-fight. Sometimes a veteran, keener-sighted than his fellows, swooped down to the ground and caused a straying mouse to struggle piteously as it felt the horn nippers closing on its back.

The moon hid herself behind a rampart of clouds, peeping with cusp or middle through

some crevice so that she might behold the
world in secret. She foresaw a tragi-comedy in
Peakland, and sent down only one sharp ray to
light the scene.

It was the twentieth anniversary of the fatal
night of Elizabeth Palfrey's life. She was
sitting by the fireside in the big parlour of the
farmhouse, striving to interest her grown-up
daughter Mary in the pictures of an old chap-
book which had belonged to her great-grand-
mother. The roughly-coloured plates and scant
letterpress told the story of " Master Dove and
His Friends," and one might read there of
palaces in hollowed rocks and of magic seas
that lay concealed in the heart of the moorland. But Mary could not understand, for,
although she was finely developed and comely
to perfection, her brain was as that of a child
in the third year. All she said was: " Mam,
mam, mam," reiterated in such a heartless way
that any stranger would have sickened with the
very sound.

The clock, whose ticking grew loud and soft,
loud and soft, so that drowsy folk would have
imagined the continuous approach and passing
of horsemen, wheezed heavily and then struck
ten, and Elizabeth closed the book.

" Et's yo'r bedtime, deary," she said. " Coom,
we'll go naa." ˙

The girl said " Mam, mam " again, and put

her soft white hand in her mother's, and together they went up the creaking staircase. On the landing Mary paused; in the candlelight Elizabeth saw her great blue eyes sparkle.

"What es et, loove?" she inquired.

Mary looked up painfully, as if something were struggling in her mind. It was very seldom that she spoke sensibly, and each time her mother was filled with a fallacious hope.

"Why doesna mam wear a ring like other grown-up women?" she stammered.

Elizabeth grew very pale and her heart leaped painfully beneath her tight brown bodice.

"Mam could weer a ring ef hoo wished," she replied in a low voice. "Mam doesna wish."

The girl began to sing "La, la, la," and they entered the chamber, where Elizabeth undressed her and helped her to don her dainty nightgown with its richly embroidered breast and wristlets, and bathed her hands in the wonderful golden hair that fell in such sweet showers. Then she put her in bed and sat by her side until she fell asleep.

The clock groaned again and struck eleven, and Elizabeth stole downstairs.

"I couldna sleep ef I tried," she said. "I mun just go an' watch for him as I've watched every year sin', an' ef I see him again, I'll ask God to curse him for what he browt on me."

She drew the fire together and took her cloak and went out into the garden. At the wicket that opened to the avenue she stood for a while, striving to pierce the gloom. The horn of the laughing moon still peeped from the chink in her fortress wall. The air had grown chill, and Elizabeth tied the strings of her cloak.

"I'll go daan to th' röad," she said. "He might pass withaat me knowin', an' I dunna wish that to be. He mun hear what I've got to say."

Then she hurried down the path, where the trees still dropped water on her uncovered head, and soon reached the great white gate that opened to the disused turnpike. The owls still fluttered to and fro, but she had been used to them all her life, and they did not even startle her.

An obsession came to her as she laid her hands on the topmost rail, and rested her forehead, waiting and trying to hear above the murmur of the rillocks — to hear the sound of someone's approach. Her breath came quick and all her body trembled. She strove to control herself, ineffectually, but all the years seemed to have rolled away and left nought in her little world save the turmoil of delight. Even Mary was forgotten — it was as if Elizabeth were in her ripe maidenhood again.

The interest of the moon became so great that she thrust aside her curtain and cast all her light into the valley. A man rode slowly along the grass-grown road. The tired horse was a powerful chestnut; its mouth was dropping flakes of foam, and its head hung almost between its forelegs. Its flanks and the steel spurs of the rider were stained with blood.

The man was drunk; he knew nothing of his whereabouts until he saw the woman who leaned against the gate, watching him with upturned face.

"By God, Bess!" he muttered. "What 's brought me here of all places to-night?"

Then he dug the spurs into the quivering flesh, but the mare refused to move. Elizabeth's memory returned; she lifted the heavy latch and passed to the middle of the road. Her hood fell back, uncovering a grey head and a frowning brow.

"Et were i' yo'r fate to coom," she said. "I 've been fain to meet yo' for mony a year, an' naa I 've gotten my desire."

But as her eyes fixed themselves on him, she saw that he was still handsome as of old, for time, having no spite against him, had touched him with kindly hands. The moonlight showed her the purely - shaped oval face, the twisted moustache, the soft effeminate mouth, and although her heart was still hardened, she could not curse.

The mist of intoxication swam before his gaze; hovering here and there he saw the rosy face of a beautiful girl smiling from wind-blown russet ringlets. The riding-whip fell to the ground; his hands were outstretched to clasp, but they fenced foolishly with empty air.

"Come nearer, Bessie," he whispered, pleadingly. "A little nearer. I must have taken too much wine at Bakewell. Don't be hard on a lad just because he's market-merry. See, I've brought you a silk handkerchief." He fumbled in his pockets. "Damn!" he exclaimed; "it's gone. I must have lost it on the way. Now, do forgive me; can't a lad drink now and again?"

A woful sigh crept from Elizabeth's lips; he heard and laughed painfully.

"I can't bear my Bess to be in trouble," he said. "Tell me what's wrong?"

Then came a sound of sobbing, and in the agony of his rejuvenated heart, he let himself down from the saddle and stumbled towards her to take her in his arms and kiss away her tears. But Elizabeth glided aside and passed through the gateway, then leaned again with her arms on the topmost bar.

He reeled forward and caught her elbows in his palms and brought his face very close to hers. She was weeping silently now: her tears fell heavily on his sleeve.

"Tell me, Bess, darling, have they been hard
on you at home again? I can't stand their
abusing you. Let us go away together."

Elizabeth cried out hysterically and held her
face so that the moonlight revealed the havoc
that her years of trouble had made.

"Yo've forgot everything! Et's a lifetime
sin' yo' spoke to me like that!"

He fell back in amazement, mumbling foolish
apologies. After a few moments he came back
again and put his hands on her shoulders. Her
flesh thrilled at the touch.

"I've hed a hard time to beer," she whispered,
hoarsely; "an' I cem to curse yo', but I canna
do et. Leave me be an' dunna coom this way
again. I've waited for yo' twenty year."

His throat was convulsed.

"Bess," he stammered, "let bygones be bygones. I'm free still, if you'll marry me—I'll
come back to-morrow. I'm a changed man—
I'll give our child a name."

He kissed her on the mouth, then he mounted
and rode away.

He broke his promise, of course; but the woman,
revelling in the recollections of that last meeting,
forgave without a murmur.

A fortnight afterwards he rode past her as she
walked on the highway with her daughter, but
although his mare scattered dust upon her skirt,
he gave no sign of recognition.

STUBBIN' GORSE

STUBBIN' GORSE

THE last snow had melted on the south-facing banks and here and there the gorse - clumps had put forth brilliant golden clusters. There was a planting of young spruces on the edge-side; in days to come it was to be used as a cover for pheasants, and the flowers overtopped some of the smaller trees.

Two men were stubbing with ancient-patterned hacks, the hafts of oak, black and shiny with wear. The elder worker was a stout, middle-aged keeper with broad cheeks and a broken nose and closely-shorn hair; his assistant, a lath-shapen young farmer with a long, wistful face and sparse red curls that lay dank on a high, narrow forehead.

It was dinner-time, and the keeper flung down his hack and hastening to the wall with an alacrity wondrous in one so portly, drew from a hole a bundle in a red cotton handkerchief that was tied in a complicated knot. Then he sat on a tussock of withered needle-grass and called his companion.

"Coom, Sam, an' hev a bit o' brëad an' pork. Moorhall 's killed a stunner o' Tuesday, an' I got th' sparrib. Et 's good i' sandwidges."

Sam came listlessly forward and sat at the keeper's side. He refused to partake of the food.

"I'll just rest wi' yo', William," he said; "but I'm none i' good form for eatin' to-day. Thank yo' all th' same. I do wish I could manage one, but th' seet o' mëat turns my heart."

The keeper made another attempt, but the young man was still obstinate.

"I'll tell yo' what, Sam," he said, testily. "Yo're gettin' nesh-bellied. Whatten's coom ower yo'."

As he ceased speaking, the bells of Milton Church began to ring, and immediately after the first chime the tune of *See the Conquering Hero comes* rose strident on the soft April breeze.

The keeper's ears pricked like those of a terrier.

"Theer's a weddin' i' th' village, an' th' band's playin'. Who es 't, dost know?"

"Ay," replied Sam in a broken voice. "Et's Ada Heppenstall fro' th' *Gowden Bull* an' a young chap fro' Gressbrook Dale."

He had grown very pale, and his breath came in slow gasps. The keeper thrust out a coarse brown hand and laid it on his narrow shoulder.

"Eh dear, I'd forgot!" he exclaimed. "Yo're feelin' bad, I'm afeard?"

"That's true," Sam said, faintly. "I've known abaat et sin' th' spurrins were put up, an et's bin a bad time for me. Haae'er, et'll soon be ower—what's doon canna be undone."

"I've ne'er heerd th' reets o' et, Sam?" the keeper said, inquiringly. "Were yo' i' loove wi' Ada?"

He was a merry fellow, given to stretching the long-bow occasionally, and of a curious disposition, but withal there was genuine feeling in his voice. A long time passed before Sam spoke : it seemed as if the cypresses that surrounded the tomb of his heart's desire were being cut down by a sacrilegious hand.

"I were, an' I am," he said.

The bells ceased for a while, then a merrier peal burst out and the two men turned their heads in the direction of the village. At the eastern end of the planting grew a copse of dwarfish beeches ; the autumn storms had torn out several and made a narrow glade, through which they saw the little town church and the speckled churchyard. The wedding party, all white and fawn and blue, no larger than a family of mice, was just leaving the porch. Sam began to shiver.

"I wouldna let likin' o' a woman tek howd o' me so," the keeper said. "Theer's more nor one for every lad i' England."

He spoke as one who had seen the world. In his earlier days he had been a miner, then a milkman in the county town, then an itinerant Methodist preacher. Once he had seen the sea, and once had spent three days in London, where he was escorted to the music-halls by his master's groom.

"Theer's women an' women," Sam said bitterly; "but on'y one woman for me."

L

A waggonette received the bridal party at the
lich-gate and drove away towards the *Golden Bull.*
The Milton band followed on foot, playing the
Wedding March from *Midsummer Night's Dream.*

"Et's on'y what I deserved," Sam sighed. "I've
just gone on carin' for yon wench sin' we went
to school together, but I've on'y bin a dumb
courter, an' I dunna think as hoo e'er rëally
knowed haa much I fancied her. I did all as I
could think o'—browt her presents fro' each fair
I went to an' sent 'em by post wi' 'fro' a lovin'
fren'' writ on, but I hedna courage to spëak. . . .
I've bin a fool, I hev, an' I'm payin' for et naa."

"Coom, Sam," the keeper said. "Hoo mun
hev known. Et were village talk. Hoo werena
wi'aat woman's wit. I heerd as hoo'd gi'en yo'
a sort o' promise—tuk pity on yo'r bashfulness,
so to speak, an' proffered to go wi' yo' to Baslow
Wakes."

Sam groaned loudly. "Ay, et were that as
did et," he faltered. "I were hangin' abaat the
Gowden Bull, an' I'd almost screwed up my pluck
to spëak an' hoo saw me watchin' her. My word,
but hoo were gran' that neet! Hoo'd on a white
dress—muslin et were, wi' a big yellow sash—th'
colour o' her hair—an' a gowd chain as her
feyther'd gi'en her for her losin'. . . . Hoo were
playin' th' pyano for a packman fro' Ulston, an'
he sang *Annie Laurie.* An' hoo caught my e'en—
happen et showed her summat, for when he'd

sung 'I 'll lay me daan an' dee,' hoo cem to me, i' face o' 'em all, an' asked were I goin' to Baslow Wakes? An' I stammered 'Ay,' an' then hoo says hoo were wantin' a squire. An' hoo looked at me that beautiful!"

The keeper had eaten his sandwiches, so they rose and went back to the stubbing. All afternoon the elder man ruminated on the half-told tale. Sam bore a very creditable reputation in the neighbourhood. The fifty-acre farm on the moor-side was his own property, and he had no encumbrances. He grew half-angry with the lad for his want of courage and determined to give him a round of good advice.

At four o'clock they started homewards. When they reached the narrow stile that opened to the road, he sat down on a stone.

"Yo 'll tell me th' rest afore I go ony farther," he said. "I 'm hearty sorry for yo', Sam; but I do think yo 're to bläame. An' what then—Ada invited yo' —— ?"

"Et 's th' worst part I 've got to coom to," Sam replied. "I went aaf to taan an' got a new suit o' clothes an' whate'er I needed, an' on th' day when we were to go, I dressed mysen an' went daan to th' *Gowden Bull.*"

He was silent again. "Ay, go on—go on," the keeper said, impatiently.

"I dunna know haa et were, but I felt just dazed wi' happiness. Well, when I reached the

public, theer were Dick Yellot o' Crosslow, an'
he would hev me sup wi' him. . . . An', what
wi' excitement an' pride, I tuk a drop too
much.

"Hoo cem in whilst I were drinkin', an' says,
surprised like, 'Yo' do look a swell, Mester
Furness; are yo' goin' aat wi' someone?' An' I
just smiled, for my tongue were tied as et always
were wi' her. 'I'm gettin' ready,' hoo says.
'I'm goin' to start i' half-an-hour.' An' I smiled
again. An' when hoo'd gone upstairs, I tuk
another glass.

"Th' upshot o' et were as I dunna remember
ony more, but neyther Ada nor me went to
Baslow Wakes. Dick Yellot he towd me as I got
up an' walked aat o' th' tap-room into th' road,
an' went daan o' my knees an' began's ef I were
oilin' a cart-wheel. I'd picked up a crow-feather
soomwheer, an' I worked et abaat quite nat'ral.
He said as Ada cem aat wi' a new gaan on an' a
big hat wi' orstridge plumes, an' when hoo saw
me, hoo laughed as ef I were dirt, an' flew i' a
temper an' went back to the haase an' tore off
her fine things an' chucked 'em aside. Hoo were
'shamed o' me. I heerd as hoo said afterwards
as I hed med her a by-word an' I werena fit for
owt but a suckin'-bottle!"

"Wenches do say bitin' things sometimes," the
keeper remarked, sympathetically. "My Mall
hed a tongue like a adder. I warrant, though,

Ada 'd hev forgi'en yo' ef yo 'd gone th' reet way abaat et. Why didna yo' mek et up?"

"Mek et up? I couldna! I did onct meet her on th' New Road, and hoo says, all red i' the face, 'Es th' cart goin' well, Mester Furness?' but I were that distrowt I daredna answer. So hoo tuk up wi' th' chap fro' Gressbrook Dale."

"Naa thaa 'st hed thy say, an' I 'll hev mine. Sam, yo 're a good lad; I dunna know a better nor a worthier, an' theer werena ony earthly reason why yo' shouldna hev hed Ada ef yo 'ld on'y shown a bit o' common-sense. But yo 've one fault, and that 's a big one. Et 's jee-jaw-jee-jaw wi' thee—thaa 'rt slow i' thowt as a carrier's waggon es i' motion. Yo'r motto 's 'Coom day, go day, God send Sunday'! When I were i' loove, th' blood o' my tongue pricked me to spëak to Mall—we chattered like pynots by th' haar together. Naa, ef yo 'd on'y gone to Ada afterwards, an' spoke an' med et up, hoo 'ld hev tuk yo' reet enow. My advice es, when yo 're coortin' another wench, just oppen yo'r maath an' let her know yo'r thowts abaat her. Ne'er mind ef it be truth or lies, but praise her till hoo 'll well nigh swallow owt. Een es no use. Cheer up, lad; naa hoo 's wed yo 'll soon get her aat o' yo'r mind!"

"That I shanna do," said Sam, as he took up his hack. "I 'll loove her as long as hoo lives, an' ef hoo dies afore me, I 'll lay me daan on her grave an' never move again."

JOHN WILLIAM'S DAUGHTERS

JOHN WILLIAM'S DAUGHTERS

PHŒBE FURNESS threw a handful of gravel at old Miss Barker's dormer window, and a minute afterwards the lattice swung open and a night-capped head popped out into the misty air. The young woman held up her lantern so that her face might be visible. It was thin and hatchet-shaped, and the sharp nose was red with indigestion and cold.

"Et's Phœbe, Miss Barker," she said. "I've coom to tell yo' as I fear Annie's sinkin' fast. Hoo seemed gettin' on all reet till ten o'clock, but hoo's wëak as a kittlin' naa."

"Eh dear! eh dear!" Miss Barker exclaimed. "I'll be wi' yo' very soon. Yo'd best send someone to raase yo'r feyther — et's but just, whate'er yo' hev again him, as he should know."

"I reckon theer'ld be talk ef I didna," Phœbe said, as she turned away; "but et's a hard job to gi'e in. We offert him his choice 'twixt us an' poachin', an' he stuck to poachin'. Haasoe'er I'd best let him know."

She disappeared in the darkness and Miss Barker began to dress quickly.

"Them Methody wenches es hard as flints," she muttered. "Et'ld on'y serve 'em reet ef

poor John William didna coom.   Ay, but he
will coom, tho', for spite o' theer whimsies he's
fond o' 'em as e'er!' "

In a short time she had reached the house,
with its little shop window dimly lighted by the
glow of a slack fire.   A half-finished gown, which
Phœbe had been sewing during the day, lay
folded on the work table.   There was no sound
save the moving of feet in the upper chamber.
As Miss Barker fastened the sneck, Phœbe came
downstairs.

"Well, yo' hevna bin long," she said.   "Hoo's
still the same.   I sent Yellot's lad up to th'
Edge for feyther.   He'll be here soon enaa."

" I'm glad yo're hevin' him, Phœbe," the old
woman said.   " I mind when yo'r mother were
i' th' same case an' he turned th' doctor aat o'
th' haase an' med summat as browt her raand
i' a day or two.   I've forgot what et were he
did, but yo' mun get him to try et.   Yo'r
mother were subject to these nervous fevers—
I reckon poor Annie's got 'em fro' her."

She went upstairs and looked at the sick
woman, gaunt and cadaverous, behind the red
curtains of the four-post bed.   To all appearance she was lifeless, but when Miss Barker
touched her pulse she found it stirring faintly.

"Hev' yo' sent for th' doctor, Phœbe?" she
whispered.

"No, I hevna.   He said as he couldna be o'

use ef hoo sank again. Th' 'stifficate 'll be all reet. Mester Green cem in an' prayed wi' her for two haars i' th' even, an' hoo seemed at rest."

As she spoke someone tapped lightly at the house-place door, and she hastened downstairs. A boy was standing outside.

"I've been up to Bretton Nook," he said, "an' raased Mr Furness, an' he says he'll be wi' yo' abaat four o'clock wi' summat as'll bring her raand. Yo're to gi'e her brandy every five minutes."

"Humph!" exclaimed Phœbe, half to herself. "Like enaa when Annie an' me's kep' th' pledge for fifteen years! Hoo'ld ne'er forgi'e me ef I touched her lips wi' that poison. Well, thank yo' for goin', Job, loove. I'll find a penny for yo' when next I see yo'."

She returned to the chamber and sat with Miss Barker at the bedside.

"Et's very hard," she grumbled, "as feyther's ways arena as aar ways. Ef he hadna bin sent to jail abaat the squire's pheasants, we couldna hev renaanced him, but that stood i' aar way i' gettin' gentlefowks' custom. We've doon twice as well sin' we cut him off. Deary me, ef Annie goes, I'll hev to tek a partner into th' business!"

Miss Barker said nothing, but sat, with compressed lips, ministering to the unconscious woman.

"I'm none sayin' owt again his bein' a kind parent," Phœbe continued. "He were sillily kind—he'd hev spoilt us wi' lettin' us hev aar own way, but we were too sensible. Mester Green uphowded us i' leavin' him when he wouldna' turn fro' his evil courses. Th' Bible becked us up."

At four oclock John William came.

"Yo' go to th' door, Miss Barker, ef yo' please," Phœbe said. "Happen I might be tempted to call him ef I did."

So the old maid went down the creaking stairs and let in the father. He was a thin gaffer, with a cleanly cut face and an abundance of bushy white hair. His eyes were red, as if he had been weeping.

"Et's yo', 'Lizbeth!" he said. "Haa's my poor dowter?"

"Abaat the same, John William," she replied. "Doff yo'r cap an' coom to th' chamber."

"I'll ne'er forget th' goodness yo've always showed to me an' mine, 'Lizbeth," he remarked. "Yo've bin a frien' o' frien's. See" (he held up a jug, swathed in flannel so that the contents might be kept hot), "I've made th' gran' med'cine I cured my wife wi', an' I pray as et'll hev th' same effect on Annie."

He followed her to the bedside, where Phœbe acknowledged his presence with a sour nod, which, however, as his eyes were still dimmed, he construed into an affectionate greeting.

"Ey, Phœbe, yo've sent for th' owd chap at last," he said, tenderly; "I knew as yo' hadna th' heart to keep him away for always."

But Phœbe rose and left them, and the poacher handed the jug to Miss Barker and knelt at the bedside, and with a silver teaspoon which he had brought, began to pour drops of the succulent elixir between his daughter's lips. She swallowed feebly, and after a while her eyelids were raised and she gazed at him vacantly,

"Et's me, Nan; et's yo'r poor owd feyther coom to gi'e beck health and strength to yo'. Naa, dunna speak, loove; lie still as a maase an' drink an' drink till yo're full. Et's what I gev to yo'r mother when hoo were bad like this."

Soon Annie petulantly turned away her face, as if the sight of him were distasteful. He shifted the candle that stood on the dressing table.

"Et's the leet as hurts her e'en, 'Lizbeth," he said. "Hoo mun be kep' as quiet as hoo can. I reckon all'll go well. I'll go whöam an' coom after breakfus', just for to see haa things es goin' on. I'm loth to turn aat, for et's comfortable in hither, an' up at the Nook a man's alöan wi' his own thowts. I'll leave th' drink for yo' to gi'e her."

Miss Barker's heart was so full that she could scarce speak distinctly.

"I'm sorry for yo', John William, very sorry," she murmured. "Et esna nat'ral for a man to live so much by himsen. Well, good-morn; happen I'll see yo' again soon."

Phœbe did not speak as he passed her in the house-place. In another minute he was groping his way through the mist up the steep and stony lane that led to his home. The old maid came downstairs soon, and laid her hand kindly on Phœbe's arm.

"I'm 'feard yo' werena as good as yo' owt to be to yo'r feyther," she said. "Save for his one fault o' poachin' (an' that he canna help) he's as noble a man as e'er breathed."

The younger woman's patience gave way. "Ef yo' think so," she retorted, "why didna yo' wed him years ago when he asked yo'. Maybe *yo'* could hev winked at his thievin' o' game! The Bible says: 'Thou shaltna steal.'"

"Ay, et does," said Miss Barker, quietly; "an' et says 'Honour thy feyther,' an' yo're breakin' that commandment every day o' yo'r life. Haasoe'er I'm none goin' to hev words wi' yo' while Annie's so badly—we'll hev et aat afterwards."

She returned to the chamber and administered more of John William's medicine to the invalid.

Phœbe came in and out without deigning to inquire concerning her sister's progress.

At ten o'clock John William appeared again, and his hale daughter met him on the thresh-hold with a suave, smiling face, and a voice like a wood-dove's.

"What were et as yo' gev poor Annie?" she inquired. "I'ld like to know, so as to be able to get her th' same i' future."

John William laughed nervously as he moved towards the staircase. "I'd best aat wi' et, wench," he said. "When yo'r mother were bad i' th' same way, I tuk my gun an snapped a brace o' cock pheasants an' plucked 'em an' stewed th' essence aat o' 'em till et were as thick as jilly. . . . As luck 'ld hev et, I'd two i' th' pantry when word cem o' my lass bein' ill, so I did the same wi em'. Et's cock pheasant broth."

Phœbe drew herself to her full height and stood, in tragical attitude, pointing to the door.

"Aat yo' go, owd man," she snarled. "Aar roof shanna coover a reprobate like yo'. Yo've browt shame and disgrace on us wi' yo'r poachin' e'er sin' I can rec'lect!"

On the evening of the same day, Miss Barker put on her cloak and overshoes and went up to John William's cottage. She found him sitting before the fire, with his chin resting on his hands.

"Yo 've bin hardly dealt wi', John William," she said, "an' I 've felt sorry for yo'. Annie 's gettin' better, so yo' need fret no more abaat her."

She poked the coals till a bright blaze danced up the chimney.

"Et 's good o' yo' to coom," he said, feebly.

'Lizabeth put her arm round his neck. "John William," she said, in a high-pitched, vibrating voice. "John William, yo' onct asked me to marry yo', an' I said nay, for I didna think yo' were as high-minded as yo' are. Yo' want someone to look after yo', so I 've coom up to say yes."

She stooped and kissed his wrinkled forehead.

OLD MAID BAMBER

M

OLD MAID BAMBER

SHE lived in a little house beyond the Nether End of Milton, a quaint, pretty place, covered with ivy and Virginia creeper. It was her own property, and the desire of her heart was to keep up the reputation for good management which her mother, who was a "foreigner" from the Yorkshire Wolds, had acquired amongst the rough-and-ready Peaklanders. For the sake of the traditions attached to her birthplace she had sacrificed a large proportion of her income, so that no damp might enter through crevices in the roughly stuccoed walls, or woodwork decay with the soft black worm.

The exterior was a miracle of neatness. A square court-garden in front sloped down to the road, traversed by narrow, box-edged paths that separated luxurious beds of sweet-williams and lupins and lad's-love. An arbour of lattice-work and hops stood like a watch-tower in a raised corner; there Old Maid Bamber used to sit in the afternoons, knitting and watching the folk pass to and from the fields, and occasionally casting proud glances at her Dutch toy mansion.

She was the wonder and the terror of the Milton women. Men upheld her as the perfect housewife of the country-side; indeed there was once talk, amongst the more erudite, of styling her home the Eighth Wonder of the Peak. To children she had a deep and apparently unconquerable aversion; at times even the approach of one of the more tiresome would cause her to tremble and flush with anger.

It was after the return of William Townend from his twenty years' absence in Canada that the spinster was brought most conspicuously into notice. There was a legend that he and she had once been engaged to be married, and that she had jilted him because he had entered her parlour with muddy feet. Such as, in past days, had known some degree of intimacy with Miss Bamber, declared that she had a wedding gown of pale green silk—the skirt bell-shaped for the fashionable crinoline—and a drawn white bonnet and a mantilla of rose-pink poplin, embroidered richly with violets and anemones, all stored away in a dower chest at the head of the narrow oaken staircase.

On the night of William Townend's home-coming, before he discovered himself to his fellow-natives, he sat in the bar-parlour of the *Golden Bull*, posing like the mysterious stranger of fiction, who eventually shines as the wealthy son or brother of the ruined lord of the manor. He was a tall, black-bearded man, with sparkling eyes and bottle-shaped nose. His well-cut clothes

concealed in some measure the Peakland slouch,
and his hands and waistcoat were embellished
with costly jewellery.

He had taken his seat amongst the crowd of
topers, and excited their admiration by ordering
quarts of the best beer all round. Sarah Heppenstall, the hostess, agog with delight at such a
customer, stood with fat, speckled arms akimbo
near the door, so overcome as to be almost incap-
able of doing his bidding. Some meaning looks
from the company, however, brought her to herself, and she hurried to the cellar.

"Hev yo' bin i' these parts afore, mester?"
Drabble of Shepherd's Farm inquired. "Yo'
seem to howd wi' good customs."

"Ay, I've been here before. Time changes
a man. I remember you ploughing against Tom
Winterton at the Noe Valley Fair."

Sarah returned and poured the beer into the
blue-and-white pots, and all nodded to the
stranger before burying their noses in the froth.
Whilst they were sighing happily after the first
draught, he rose and caught up his coat tails
and stood with his back to the low fire.

"As I said, I've been here before," he continued. "More than any of you are thinking
of. I won't tell you my name — you must find
it out for yourselves. I hadn't a beard in
those days. . . . I thought, since I'd made
my pile, I'd come back and look up a few old

friends. Is Job Robinson of Cockey Lowe living yet?"

"Dëad, mester, last New Year's E'en; he were ower ninety year owd."

"And Emma Bamber of Hollowbrook Cottage —who did she marry?"

A laugh came from the younger men. "Owd Maid Bamber!" Drabble exclaimed. "Hoo's ne'er wedded, an' ne'er bin like to wed for mony a long year as I know on!"

The stranger's face flushed deeply. "Why, I think I remember some talk of her court-ing with William Townend," he said, with an affectation of carelessness. "It never came off, then?"

"None so. They quarrelled abaat his shoon bein' dirty—he'd gone to see her after muckin' th' shippons, wi'aat cleanin' 'em on th' grass, an' hoo tuk offence. Fowk say as hoo regretted et, for he went away, an' hoo ne'er heerd owt o' him again. A fine chap were William, tall an' limber as a kecksie! Owd Maid ne'er were th' same after he went; first thing hoo did, tho' hoo were but a wench hersen, were to tek against childern. Hoo'd always bin' very fond o' 'em afore, but sin' hoo'd resolved, so to spëak, none to marry an' hev soom o' her own, hoo couldna beer th' seet o' other fowk's. Hoo's wild as a hornet e'en ef a little un chucks a stöane into her garden, an' theer's mothers i' Milton as declare hoo keeps a

pot o' boilin' wayter on th' hob to scald bäirns
wi' ef they worry her. Et 's but a tale."

"I knew her well," the stranger remarked,
"and I can't believe as she 's really turned out
that way. She used to be the kindest and the
prettiest girl in the Peak."

Suddenly Mrs Heppenstall's empty pitcher fell
to the floor and broke into fragments.

"Et 's William—William Taanend himsen!"
she cried. "Coom back a gentleman!"

The stranger laughed boisterously, and without waiting for any felicitations, ordered another
serving of quarts and, dropping a sovereign into
her hand, passed out hastily into the twilight.
When he had reached the Nether End, he turned
up the lane that led to Hollowbrook, and sitting
on a low wall, unlaced his great boots and put on
a pair of patent leather slippers. Then, carrying
the boots in one hand, he opened the gate of
Old Maid Bamber's garden, and went up timidly
to the white door.

He tapped thrice, but nobody came. After
he had rested for some time on the bench, his
heart heavy with fear lest she had seen and
refused to admit him, an old woman came past.

"Ef yo 're wantin' Miss Bamber," she said,
"hoo 'll be here i' abaat an haar. Hoo 's gone
up wi' soom broth to John Yellot at th' Moor-
gate,—him as es laid up wi' rheumatise."

She went on, and still he sat. After the church

clock had struck nine, however, it occurred to him to make a journey of inspection, and he started by trying the door-sneck. By some unwonted carelessness she had forgotten to take the key, so he entered the cottage and sat down in the big arm-chair by the parlour window, where posies of lilac in big brown jars diffused a divine fragrance.

An odd fancy came to him and he carried his boots to the house-place, and set them on the broad bar of the fender and poked the coals till they blazed brightly; then he returned to the parlour.

Old Maid Bamber came in at ten o'clock, aghast to find that she had left the door unfastened. When she saw the boots she gave a wild and painful cry.

"Theer's bin a ghöast here! They're Bill's, my lad Bill's. Nob'dy i' th' lond had feet that shäape an' size!"

He stole behind her and caught her in his arms.

"Emma, wench," he said, his speech losing the refinement which a broader life had given. "I've coom to ask yo' again. I've never sin ony as I could care for but yo'!"

Despite the fact that she was nearly fainting, Old Maid Bamber turned round and bussed him passionately on the mouth.

"I were a fool to send yo' away, Bill," she panted. "I surely didna deserve a thowt!"

"Ay, but yo' did, yo' were i' th' reet. I'd no business coomin' i' them mucky shoon. See what I've got on naa."

But her eyes were so dim with tears that she distinguished nought save two objects like tea-trays glittering on the hearth.

"I'm rich, Em. Yo've to share wi' me all I've addled. Let's be wed at onct."

. . . .

A miracle happened. Mrs Townend's antipathy to children passed away within the first year of her marriage. Village folk were incredulous at first, but the report of its removal proved well-founded. Besides making her William (in his own estimation) the happiest man in the world, she did him the honour of presenting him with a fine boy and girl—the boy being the elder by five minutes. These reign in arbitrary fashion over the Steeple House—that mansion near the church, which William gave Emma for a bridal offering — and upset all their mother's neat domestic arrangements.

Gossip says that she is about to give a grand children's party, at which every infant in the neighbourhood is to be present, and that the little Emma will wear a gown made of an old-fashioned rose-pink mantilla, embroidered with violets and anemones.

N

www.ingramcontent.com/pod-product-compliance
Lightning Source LLC
Chambersburg PA
CBHW030557040726
47497CB00008B/2772